By H. R. F. Keating

Mystery Novels

BATS FLY UP FOR INSPECTOR GHOTE
DEATH & THE VISITING FIREMEN
INSPECTOR GHOTE TRUSTS THE HEART
INSPECTOR GHOTE GOES BY TRAIN
INSPECTOR GHOTE BREAKS AN EGG
INSPECTOR GHOTE PLAYS A JOKER
INSPECTOR GHOTE HUNTS THE PEACOCK
INSPECTOR GHOTE CAUGHT IN MASHES
INSPECTOR GHOTE'S GOOD CRUSADE
IS SKIN DEEP, IS FATAL
THE PERFECT MURDER
DEATH OF A FAT GOD
THE DOG IT WAS THAT DIED
A RUSH ON THE ULTIMATE
ZEN THERE WAS MURDER

Novel

THE STRONG MAN

BATS FLY UP
FOR
INSPECTOR GHOTE

BATS FLY UP
FOR
INSPECTOR GHOTE

H. R. F. KEATING

27313

PUBLISHED FOR THE CRIME CLUB BY
DOUBLEDAY & COMPANY, INC.
GARDEN CITY, NEW YORK
1974

All of the characters in this book
are fictitious, and any resemblance
to actual persons, living or dead,
is purely coincidental.

Library of Congress Cataloging in Publication Data

Keating, Henry Reymond Fitzwater, 1926–
    Bats fly up for Inspector Ghote.
    I. Title.
PZ4.K253Bat3   [PR6061.E26]   823'.9'14
ISBN 0-385-05859-4
Library of Congress Catalog Card Number 74–3527

Copyright © 1974 by H. R. F. Keating
All Rights Reserved
Printed in the United States of America
First Edition in the United States of America

BATS FLY UP
FOR
INSPECTOR GHOTE

I

Till the bats begin to fly. Inspector Ghote set that time as
a limit. Within a few minutes of the creatures coming, swooping
and darting over the heads of the crowds beginning now to saun-
ter up from Chowpatty Beach, darkness would be on them all, like
a lid swiftly placed down. And then there would be no hope at
all of spotting a pickpockets' team.

Then there would be no chance, as a gang made its way pur-
posefully along against the stream of festival-happy, homeward-
bound Bombayites, of ambushing one of them just at the moment
of his crime. Then there would be no more chances of notching
up just one more arrest towards the secret total which, Ghote suspected uneasily, Deputy Superintendent Samant had set for him.
And the cloud of faint disgrace which he felt hung round him always nowadays would become one shade darker. He could not
afford to let that happen.

When the bats left their daytime hanging-places, perhaps in the
trees round Blavatsky Lodge just back from the sweep of Marine
Drive, perhaps in the gardens beside the much-domed Babulnath
Temple, it would be too late. Ghote scanned the crowd, with
which he was slowly moving onwards, almost feverishly.

The people strolling alongside him were nearly shoulder-to-
shoulder thick as far ahead as he could see. Thousands and thousands had come down to Chowpatty's broad semicircle of sand
to watch the final ceremonies of the Ganpati Festival on its
twelfth and last day. The earlier events had not attracted so much
attention, but the final ceremony was, as always, the occasion for
immense excitement.

As many as a hundred thousand people had been expected to
line the routes of the processions taking the huge decorated statues of elephant-headed Lord Ganesha, mounted on slowly chug-

ging trucks, down to the shores of the city to be immersed in the sea. Balconies all along the routes had been packed to danger point. Pavements had been jammed to stifling closeness. The branches of the trees had been loaded with ambitious urchins, shouting and bright-eyed. And then, when the holy idols and the floats with scenes from the Ramayana and the Mahabharata and the marchers from the poorer quarters with their homemade music and their gymnastic displays had gone by, all the watchers, elated by their darshan of pot-bellied, luck-bringing Lord Ganesha, had come pouring down to the beaches. And there the gorgeous statues, gold and silver and mirror-brilliant embroidery outside, clay or plaster within, had gone lurching inch by inch into the consuming sea.

It had all meant more work for the Police Department, leave forbidden, extra hours meted out.

But thanks to them the whole business had been orderly and peaceful. The lost children had been taken to the specially setup collection points and had eventually been restored to distraught parents. The people who had fainted had been carried to the first-aid stations. Potential rioters had seen the signs and had behaved themselves. And, if pockets had been picked in these ideal conditions, arrests had equally been made.

It had been police work at its best. Ghote felt a solid contentment at the thought of it all. Except that by no means enough of the pickpocketing arrests had been made by him. He needed more. Ideally several more. One more at least definitely, before darkness fell.

Well, the circumstances could not be better for him. A pickpocketing gang would stand out here clearly as clearly, despite all the thousands of people. To a mind tuned to see the pattern of men or boys, each on his own, making their way against the stream of a crowd, nothing could be clearer. It would be unmistakable to the properly suspicious eye. There would be the leader, the one who made the actual thefts, with close behind him the handover wallah, to receive the stolen purses or wallets within moments of the lifting. And then in a looser chain behind there would be another two or three gang members to pass the booty swiftly along till in one rapid inconspicuous movement it would be safe to gut the contents, throw away the incriminating container and pass back the money. And somewhere to the side—it would have been on the opposite pavement if the road was narrower than the broad sweep here—there would be the lookout, eyes darting to and fro, terribly obvious to the trained mind in his contrast to the easygoing holidaymakers all round.

A lookout would show up, no doubt, as much as he himself would show up to them, pricklingly alert as they must be, if he were not constantly making sure his every glance was under control. Or as much as Acting Detective-Constable D'Cruz, his Anglo-Indian partner in this weary chore, must show up. And, following at a regulation twenty-five yards' distance, he would be jutting up like a great, bandaged, sore thumb.

D'Cruz was a trial. And, Ghote suspected at times, a trial deliberately thrust upon him by Deputy Superintendent Samant himself. It was necessary to have two officers in tandem on anti-pickpocketing duties, since seldom does the victim know that a theft has taken place at all and thus can never be relied on as a witness, but as a second man D'Cruz was useless.

It was not that he did not see things. On the contrary, he saw too much. Anything and everything was liable to distract him. A pretty girl student, long plait of hair swinging, or a particularly ugly old woman, face hair-sprouting and gap-toothed, lined with wrinkles close as they could cram, either was likely to catch his eye and hold him gawping. A one-eyed man, an ash-smeared sadhu, a tall-turbaned Rajput, any such moderately common sight might halt him in his tracks and put him into a daze of unthinking wonder.

Plain then to see how, with such a Number Two, his tally of arrests had been so low in all the months that he had day after day been allocated to this most chore-like of detective duties. And how could he not help suspecting that D'Cruz was part of some scheme of the DSP's. Was it not being made almost impossible for him to show good results so that he could be eased out of the CID without having grounds for complaint?

But surely that was ridiculous? Surely he must be seeing plots where none existed? After all, someone had to be put on anti-pickpocketing patrol. And someone, even, since D'Cruz had been admitted on probation to the CID, had to show the chap the ropes.

But he must not let thoughts like these blossom in his head. They obscured concentration.

All too easily it was possible to let the mind wander. And then all that met the eye was people, people of all sorts, milling happily along, men, women, and children. Then boys on their own looked simply like sportive youngsters dashing away from family groups. Then you stopped seeing that some of them were hardened little trained criminals. Then you forgot that homeless urchins were recruited by the bosses of the pickpocketing gangs. You forgot there were boys who, in return for being housed and fed and with the fear of punishment and of deprivation goading them sharply on, went out to rob just as hard as they could by day and by night.

Boys on the night shifts would be beyond his catching, except by some lucky accident. But the daytime operators, working in that giveaway pattern, he should be able to pick up one of those still. One at least. He must.

He squared his bony shoulders and sent his gaze roaming systematically over the mass of humanity moving in front of him. He sought the telltale signs from among all the men in white shirts and white trousers, the men in coloured shirts and dhotis, the men in floppy kurtas and baggy pyjama, the women in every colour and pattern of holiday sari, the children in shorts or in frocks, trailing along, half delighted and half overwhelmed by all the press and all the noise.

And, yes, surely . . . Yes. There. There was a face he knew. The fellow was, unless he was mistaken, the boss of one of the smaller child gangs, a well-known pickpocket though he himself had yet to pull him in.

Yes, Moti Chiplunkar. The name floated to the front of Ghote's mind from his dutiful poring over the cards in Records.

He looked hard at the figure some twenty-five or thirty yards off, working its way towards him in an apparently casual manner. A short squat body clad in a greasy-looking red checked shirt and a pair of dark trousers. A round much-wrinkled face, looking incredibly aged though the hair above it was glossy and black. Moti Chiplunkar, a seasoned monkey.

No doubt he was out with a party of boys from his gang, keeping an eye on them or perhaps taking a hand himself amid the rich pickings of Ganpati Day. Most probably he was acting as lookout. So there ought to be a line of predatory boys to be seen to the side of him, though they would not have much room to work with the sea wall so close.

No. No, that was not this particular pattern after all. There. It was clearly to be seen, spaced out behind Chiplunkar himself. That boy in the torn green shirt. And, six or seven yards past him, a bigger boy in a dirty white singlet, with, farther back, the boy in the red shirt. And, yes, even surely that tiny figure, peering ahead in solid concentration, probably not more than seven years of age, in some sort of pinkish undervest much too big for him.

So Moti Chiplunkar himself must be the lifter today.

Ghote, turning his head a little away and endeavouring more than ever to put on an air of holiday fecklessness, kept the pick-pocket under unremitting scrutiny. He felt, pulsing through him now, the tingling excitement of the hunt. It was always like that when suddenly the wearing routine became transformed into ac-tive chase. Abruptly everything was simplified. It was himself, the hunter, and whoever it was he was hunting. Nothing else mat-tered.

D'Cruz, somewhere behind, ceased at once to be a possible burden deliberately imposed by DSP Samant. Instead, he became simply a factor to be kept in mind in the scheme of the hunt, a weakness that had to be taken into account. He was just the same as any other unalterable factor, the nearness of the sea wall or some particular home-going festival watcher—that plump woman in the light green muslin sari: "Move, fat pig"—who might or might not get between him and his target.

And then, quite suddenly, the moment came.

When Ghote was still about five yards away from Moti Chip-lunkar, and well to the side of him, the shifting bodies in the crowd abruptly rearranged themselves. And they presented the pick-pocket with a chance he must have seen as heaven-sent. Ghote was able to observe it all. A big fat man with depressed-looking, sloping shoulders under his white shirt and broad elephant-like hips in baggy grey trousers had drifted right into Chiplunkar's path. And, actually jutting out of the hip pocket of the trousers, there was a crammed wallet. A little foam of white notes rimmed its bright brown leather.

Ghote watched Chiplunkar complete his final manoeuvrings for the swoop. To the casual onlooker there would have been nothing to see. But to the eye that was properly suspicious the meaning of the slight changes in body position, of the manner in which the arms were being swung, was as clear to interpret as the measured-to-a-finger's-breadth gestures of a Kathakali dancer.

And, yes, Ghote said to himself with a licking inner joy, I shall be in just the right place to grab the fellow with the wallet still in his fingers. Just right.

Then, abruptly as the pattern had formed, it changed. Beside the elephant-hipped man with the generous wallet his wife had been moving along with the crowd, a shorter, rather stiff figure in a sari of sober grey scarcely relieved by neat blue squares. On her arm was a round open basket containing the remains of a picnic. And, at almost the moment that Moti Chiplunkar had been going to pounce, a darting boy, attracted by the sound of rough music down on the sands below, had raced forward and had just tipped the back edge of the basket. Jolted from it had come a small but thick little black-bound wallet.

Ghote saw Moti Chiplunkar hesitate. He felt he could read the very thoughts in his mind. To ignore this chance, and to work his way again behind Elephant Hips with that obvious supply of crammed notes? Or to grab what the gods had just put straight in front of him, the prize without difficulties but perhaps without great value?

The hesitation was only momentary. A man who has plied the pickpocket's trade over the years has a quick mind.

Moti Chiplunkar swiftly stooped and in one rapid scooping motion gathered up the black wallet. And as quickly, Ghote dived.

He flung himself across the path of some holidaymakers and clamped his left hand firmly round the pickpocket's thin wiry wrist. And at the same time he called loudly to the owner of the black wallet. "Madam, madam." Identification of the stolen object would be an important factor in making sure a charge stuck. And where was Constable D'Cruz? Had he witnessed what had occurred?

But the victim was walking steadily away with her heavy-hipped husband beside her, both oblivious of any extra noise amid the loud voices and the laughter all around. And D'Cruz? Ghote saw, as he straightened up pulling the pickpocket with him, that D'Cruz was a good fifty yards away, standing still, gawping down at the beach below. There was a troupe of acrobats at work there—it had been their drum and pipes that had attracted the darting boy—and such a sight could not but hold a fellow like D'Cruz lost in mind-absorbing fascination as a pole-grasping figure swayed and swung along the slack rope strung between two tall bamboo tripods.

Ghote turned to his captive grimly. He was going to have to pin that charge on him by bluff. But he was going to do it. Unless he did he would miss his arrest. After this there could scarcely be time enough to spot another prospect and catch him in the act before the bats came out.

"Police, brother," he said to Chiplunkar in coarse Marathi. "You chose the wrong time for it."

The pickpocket looked up at him, his seamed monkey face bitter.

"You must be the new anti-pickpocket," he said. "Or I'd have seen you coming. Who are you?"

"I have been on it three months," Ghote answered. "Long enough to know all about you. And I am Inspector Ghote, as you will find out when you come up before a Presidency Magistrate tomorrow."

"Three months," Moti Chiplunkar said, a look of speculation coming to his age-old face. "Three months, and you have not yet learnt the difference between stealing and returning *loss prarparti.*"

The last two words were in English, or in Chiplunkar's thick version of it. And with them a sudden lead weight sank down through Ghote's being.

He knew that the pickpocket was trying it on. He had seen on the wizened monkey-visage the notion forming itself of attempting to persuade this newcomer to anti-pickpocketing duties that he had slipped up. But he also knew that what had been said represented nothing less than the truth. Chiplunkar could have been simply picking up the black wallet with the intention of restoring it to its owner. There was no proof that he had not been going to do exactly that.

Equally, of course, there was no proof that, two seconds before his thin long thief's fingers had caught up the fallen wallet, he had not been going to lift a bulging note case from the back pocket of the elephant-hipped husband. There was no proof: but he knew as certainly as he knew anything that it was so.

To all intents and purposes Moti Chiplunkar was a fair catch. And he was a catch that it was very necessary for him to have.

"Loss prarparti," he echoed scornfully, letting not a tremor of his doubts show through. "You were picking up this wallet as *loss prarparti*? My friend, when I tell that Presidency Magistrate that I saw you take it and you say you picked it up off the ground, which of us is he going to believe?"

For a moment he thought he had done it: browbeaten the fellow into thinking he had no hope and might as well plead guilty and not have the police make too much of his record in court. But then a new expression of calculation came over the monkey face.

"Ghote," the pickpocket said thoughtfully. "When I heard that name I knew someone had told me something about Inspector Ghote. Ghote. Ghote is the one who never improves the evidence. Inspector, you know that I have not committed offence."

He looked up in sheerly brazen effrontery.

Ghote longed to smash his fist down on that face. And at the same time he realised that he had been paid a considerable compliment. And he relished it, for all that he had a shrewd idea that to the thief it was no praise.

By way of answer he wrenched the little, thick black wallet out of the thief's long fingers and thrust it hastily into his own empty left-hand hip pocket.

"All right," he said. "This time, go."

"Inspector," said Moti Chiplunkar, his monkey eyes glittering now with laughter, "should I not take that wallet to *Loss Prarparti* myself?"

Ghote swung a kick at his shins.

But the pickpocket saw it coming almost as soon as Ghote had lifted the sole of his foot from the ground. And, with all the adroitness of one who had made his living among crowds since he had been the merest boy, he slid sideways. In a few seconds he was lost to view among the bumbling bodies of the honest citizens of Bombay making their way homeward after watching the solemn immersion of the Ganesha idols.

Inspector Ghote looked up at the sky.

It was still unsmirched by the faintest hint of night. There was no sign of the bats. Perhaps there might yet, by some incredibly lucky chance, be time to make that one necessary arrest. Perhaps and perhaps he would yet cheat fate that had simultaneously given him the gift he so needed and prevented him from taking it. Perhaps.

He set off again moving along with the slowly progressing crowd. Heavy though the pressure of sad self-castigation was inside him, he managed nevertheless to set his mind once more into the ever-alert, sifting and analysing state that was often second nature to him.

But the bats were to fly that evening, and for many another after, without Inspector Ghote making an arrest. He had gone only some hundred yards past the spot where he had had his disastrous encounter with Chiplunkar when a quiet voice spoke into his ear.

"Inspector Ghote. Do not look round. Walk on another fifty yards, and then stop and lean on the sea wall looking down onto the beach."

II

Inspector Ghote walked on at the same loiterer's pace for half a dozen steps. Should he do what this unknown voice had told him to? Would it not be better to swing around and confront the speaker, tell him not to play stupid tricks?

Yet the voice had been so calm. The order, odd though it was, had been given so quietly, as if there could be no question of it being disobeyed. And, more, as if it was decidedly important that it should be followed out unquestioningly.

He decided there was nothing to be lost by simply doing what had been asked.

He walked on, taking what opportunities he could to get nearer to the sea wall. By the time he had gone the requested fifty yards he was right beside the waist-high wall. He drifted to a halt, turned and stood with his hands on the wall's white stone top. He looked down as if in pure idleness at the people on the soft dry sands below.

For a few seconds he waited.

Then the quiet authoritative voice spoke again.

"Good man. I was afraid you'd make a fuss."

Ghote turned his head a little. He was putting it in the lion's mouth, though he was far from knowing that then. It was his first step towards an antagonist able to inflict deeper punishment than any enemy he had yet encountered.

The person standing beside and a little behind him was the last man on earth he had expected to see. What was Mr. Rao, one of the Assistant Commissioners of his own force, doing, dressed in a mere white open-necked shirt and white slacks, here among the sweaty crowds celebrating Ganpati Day? People as exalted as Assistant Commissioners were on days such as this either in their offices, splendid and aloof, or away with their families at some secluded seaside hotel or in the cool of the hills, playing golf, say, at Mahableshwar.

Yet here beside him was that tall figure, a person so removed from the everyday hurly-burly of police work that it was only by chance that he himself had been able to put a name to the long, serious-looking, cool-eyed face with its iron-grey tuft of military moustache.

But Mr. Rao had known what he looked like.

The thought came suddenly, and at once set disquieting ideas loose in his mind. He had been picked out, noticed, pointed at. Something was in store for him. Something that it needed the full weight of an Assistant Commissioner to impose. It would not then be just dismissal from the force. If that had been decided on, DSP Samant as his present superior officer would have been perfectly capable of informing him. No, perhaps there was to be an inquiry of some sort. An inquiry going to the very roots of the force, and that was why whatever it was had become an Assistant Commissioner level matter. He was going to be asked to plead guilty so that things to the discredit of the force would not come into the open. But guilty to what? What had he done?

"I thought I was never going to get you on your own, Ghote," Mr. Rao said, the words dropping into the whirlpool-mad chaos of his thoughts and quieting them like an oil.

"On my own, sir?" he repeated.

"Yes. That Detective Constable with you. Never once took his eyes off you. Wouldn't have seen a pickpocket if there had been one operating under his very nose."

Well, Ghote thought, at least D'Cruz had not been gawping.

"He is fairly new on the job, sir," he said to Mr. Rao. "But I think he is learning."

"Perhaps."

Mr. Rao did not sound particularly convinced. He stared down in silence for a few moments at the beach below, still despite the numbers of the returning crowds well covered with people. Then he spoke again in the same purlingly assured voice.

"Well, the chap is happily absorbed in an acrobatic show now. So we can have a few words without me having to take you off anywhere."

"Yes, sir," Ghote said.

But what could it be that Mr. Rao wanted to speak to him about? He no longer believed he was going to hear a request to turn Approver in some case against himself and other members of the force. Mr. Rao had not sounded in any way hostile. And besides there was nothing for him to turn Approver about. So what could be coming?

Down below them the chelas of a yogi who had spent the whole day buried deep beneath the sand in honour of Lord Ganesha were making preparations to dig him up. They were spreading first a rug on which to receive cash contributions from the small circle of curious onlookers once the yogi had been seen to be fit and well.

"When you get back to your office this evening," Mr. Rao said, "you will find a memo telling you that you have been transferred."

To Traffic after all? But, no. It would need no Assistant Commissioner to seek him out amid all the Ganpati Day crowds to tell him that. So what was happening? What?

"Yes, sir?" he said, trying to force into his voice the quiet note that Mr. Rao so effortlessly achieved.

"Transferred to the Black-money and Allied Transactions Squad."

Ghote could hardly believe the words, though they had been spoken by a figure as unquestionable as Mr. Rao himself.

Black money. The sums, often huge, that people with no respect for the law deliberately put out of reach of the various tax authorities. Whether it was selling a luxury penthouse apparently at one figure but in reality for perhaps double that sum with the undeclared extra going free of any form of tax, or whether it was a film star insisting on getting a large proportion of his or her salary without anything appearing in the books so that no income tax could be demanded, or whether it was the cash used for smuggling transactions in which no part of the deal ever came out into the open, it was all the same. It was, whatever justifications might be used by those agreeing to such deals, an affront to the proper working of the nation.

And the Black-money and Allied Transactions Squad had recently been formed, of CID officers picked as being the real top-notchers, to fight the racketeers making the biggest sums out of the system. To be selected to join that: it was incredible.

Yet how he would like to be in on it, to do something, however small, to counter the men in Bombay who were callously ripping out perhaps the biggest hole in the financial fabric of the entire country. Black money was being made in lakhs and crores of rupees in the great commercial centre and through the long coast-line running from it. To be able to put a spoke in that wheel, to bring to a halt just some part of the trickery and the deceit: that would be a job worth doing.

But why him?

He acknowledged his limits. The Squad had been chosen from the very best men, and he did not think he ranked among them. He hoped he did not deserve the low opinion that DSP Samant and others had of him. But, much though he would like to be put-ting right wrongs of such magnitude, he suspected that he did not really carry enough weight to do it.

"You will be asking why it is you have been chosen for a job of this sort now," Mr. Rao said, quietly echoing his thoughts.

"Yes, sir, I was. I was asking that."

"I'm glad to hear it, Inspector. At least you have no inflated notions of your own importance."

"No, sir."

"Perhaps you've also asked yourself why I should have spent the whole of a hot and sticky Ganpati Day afternoon looking out for you."

"I had already wondered about that, sir."

"Good again. There's something to be said for an officer who asks the right questions."

Ghote savoured the crumb of praise. But against those bleak implications about his ability to combat the black-money bosses it was little enough to be grateful for.

Down on the beach the yogi's chelas had begun spading out the sand that covered him. There was a craning of heads from the onlookers, at once wanting to find the holy man alive and well and yet unwilling to believe they were not the victims of some trickery.

"Well," Mr. Rao said, "the reason for my taking this somewhat extraordinary step is simple: a most unpleasantly extraordinary situation exists."

Ghote's mind buzzed with speculation. And under the buzz he felt a deep and awful unease.

"Twice within the past fortnight," the Assistant Commissioner went on, "officers of the Black-money Squad have been about to pull off a big arrest only to find, when the trap closed, that the suspect had got clear away."

"Breach of security, sir?" Ghote asked, unable to keep his sense of shock out of his voice, naive though he felt himself to be.

"Yes, Ghote, breach of security. In a squad of officers specially selected to have intelligence enough not to go blabbing their secrets and to be beyond any possibility of corruption. You do right to look shocked."

"But, sir," Ghote said tentatively, "is it not possible that these failures were a matter of coincidence only?"

"Yes, it is possible. But if we had thought, taking into account the full circumstances of each case, that there was sufficient other explanation, I would hardly be out here talking to you now."

"No, sir."

"No. What I needed above all was an officer who was a little removed from his colleagues, who could look at them with a cold eye. And, thanks to the recent course of your career, you precisely fill that bill, Ghote."

"Yes, sir."

Darkness began to fall, the light instant by instant losing its brilliance. At a distant little bhel-puri stall down on the beach the vendor lit a flary torch.

Ghote felt a parallel darkness descending inside him. The Black-money and Allied Transactions Squad was not going to be for him the crusade he had seen it as being. It was going to be a shadowed world of meanness and spying. He glimpsed some of the things it would be necessary for him to do. He might have to peek into the circumstances of his brother officers' private lives. He would find himself testing the drawers of their desks on the chance they had left them unlocked and conducting hasty surreptitious searches. He would have to scrabble in wastepaper baskets. It would be an unsavoury business.

And he had been chosen for it, he registered, not because his abilities were being at last acknowledged, but simply because he had become an outsider. Because he was cut off from the day-to-day gossip and the common run of friendships in the CID, and for no other reason, he was being pitchforked into the terrible responsibilities ahead.

And yet . . . Yet if there had been the breaches of security that Mr. Rao was combating, then to find the man responsible would be a task worth shouldering indeed. It would still be worth doing even though, were he under Mr. Rao's tutelage actually to achieve success, in the nature of things it would never be something that brought him credit. But to do it: to root out the betrayer of all that police work stood for, it would be worth anything.

"Sir," he said to the tall quiet figure at his side, "I will altogether do my best."

"Good man, Inspector."

And suddenly in a series of jumping dazzling shocks the floodlights all along the edge of the great sweep of the beach were switched on in celebration of the day. Huge fans of garish light leapt up to send giant black pointing shadows everywhere. Behind them, as they swung round to avoid the glare, the casuarina trees reared up like monstrous menacing figures.

"Suspect everyone," the Assistant Commissioner said unruffledly. "That's your first duty, Ghote. To suspect everyone."

Then, dancing and swooping into the harsh glare of the lights, at last there came the bats from Blavatsky House and the gardens round the Babulnath Temple. Black, wide-winged, gaunt.

"Well, Inspector, welcome to the Bats."

"The Bats, DSP Naik, sir?"

Ghote blinked stupidly down at the broad round face of the Deputy Superintendent in charge of the Black-money and Allied Transactions Squad. It was the morning after his extraordinary conversation with Mr. Rao and he still felt considerably bewildered by the sudden change in the course of his life.

DSP Naik puffed out his protuberant lips under the soft blur of his moustache. Rage-blood began to gather in his cheeks.

"The Bats, man, the Bats," he said. "The Black-money and Allied Transactions Squad. BATS. Surely you must have heard us called that? Where have you been, Inspector?"

"On anti-pickpocketing patrol, DSP." Ghote answered smartly.

"I did not ask you where you were yesterday, man. I asked

where you have been in all the months since the Bats were formed."

"But it was on anti-pickpocketing patrol, DSP sahib. I have been sent out on it every day for three months and more until today."

DSP Naik blew a long stream of air through his lips. He looked increasingly puzzled. Ghote felt acutely that he was not making the good impression he had intended.

That morning he had taken particular pains to be at Headquarters a full fifteen minutes before he was due to report. And he had taken equally special care over his appearance, even though his sudden demand for a fresh pair of trousers and a clean shirt had not made him popular with his wife. Indeed, he had had to promise to wear the old trousers again in off-duty hours before she had consented to take an iron to one of his new smart pairs. Now all this careful preparation seemed to have been nullified.

"Inspector," the DSP said, looking up from his desk with the frown still etched on his round face, "I am beginning to wonder whether there has not been some mistake in posting you to us."

"Oh, no, DSP. No mistake, sir."

"And how are you so sure of that, Inspector?" the DSP pounced. "I did not apply for an increase in establishment. The first I knew of your coming was yesterday when I received a memo to that effect. Did you know earlier than that?"

Ghote felt a rising panic. Whatever he did, he must not let the DSP guess there was anything out of the way about his appointment. The DSP himself was one of those he had got to suspect. Mr. Rao had made that clear in the course of the rest of their talk in the darkness of Chowpatty Seaface the evening before. Certainly the sums at the disposal of the big black-money bosses were quite large enough to tempt even a man on a Deputy Superintendent's pay rate.

But already, within minutes of his having joined the Bats—he must, must learn to call them that—the DSP was suspecting that his posting was not all it seemed.

"Oh, no, sir, no," he stammered. "You have got altogether wrong idea, sir."

"Have I, indeed? I think not. There is something I do not at all like about your coming to us, Ghote."

"But, sir. Sir, I am posted to you only because recent operations have not been a success."

"Not a success? And tell me, Inspector, just how do you know that? The work of my Squad is Top Secret. Top Secret. And yet I find an inspector from anti-pickpocketing patrol knowing all about it. Now, how does that happen, Inspector Ghote?"

Ghote gulped.

"Sir," he said. "It is quite simple."

His brain raced.

"Sir, it was stated in the memo detailing my posting, sir."

Would the DSP ask to see the memo? Ghote waited with heart thumping.

He was spared that. But what DSP Naik did fasten onto was in a way worse.

"So, Inspector," he said, "you are given information that was intended to be confidential to myself and officers of over and above Assistant Commissioner rank. I should very much like to know how that came about, very much indeed."

"Yes, sir."

" 'Yes, sir.' 'Yes, sir.' What does that mean, Inspector?"

The DSP's eyes in his broad round face went suddenly hard.

"Favouritism," he said. "That is what it means. Well, you listen to me, Inspector Ghote. I do not care how you got into this Squad, but once you are in it you get no privileges from me. And I get no insubordination from you. Understand? So let's not have any 'Yes, sir' back answers from you."

"Yes, sir. I mean, no, sir," Ghote stammered.

But he was filled with such a sense of relief that the DSP had hit on this convenient explanation for his arrival on the Squad that his surface discomfiture bothered him not at all.

"No, Inspector, the Bats exist to beat the black-money wallahs. And we are going to do it, even if I have to work you till you are dropping."

"Yes, sir," said Ghote.

And he straightened his shoulders under his clean white shirt.

Surely, he thought, whoever it is in the Bats— Yes, the Bats— who is selling information it cannot be the DSP. A man who had always had a reputation for keenness. All that insistence on junior officers playing hockey on every possible occasion. No, it could not be the DSP. And now he seemed filled with a new zeal even. He was a crusader.

"Very well, Inspector. Come and meet your colleagues."

Ghote followed the DSP out of his office. He felt alertness pricking at every cell of his brain. The men he was about to meet were not only top-notch officers selected for their keenness and ability: one of them was, must be, a traitor of the worst sort to all that he held high.

Would he see him at once somehow? Catch, with the fresh eye of the newcomer, some tiny trick of expression? Detect with the penetrating X ray of fired suspicion some little give-away inconsistency? Would he? Could he?

He went forward eager for the fray and, for all his self-doubts, failing totally to realise how wily and how strong was the deeper-lurking antagonist he was soon to encounter.

III

The moment that Inspector Ghote entered the Bats' office, a big, cool, air-conditioned room all gleaming in new light wood and unsullied white paint, pointed in its contrast with the dark little cubbyhole and its single monotonously groaning fan that had for so long been his own, he realised that his task was going to be far harder than he had in his moment of resolution on the way in optimistically expected. There were two men at work in the room, and they were of all the officers in the CID, he thought, the two he would least have chosen to have to assess as suspects.

At the large, glossy, stainless-steel handled, ultra-efficient desk nearest the door—how it showed up his own, familiar, whorled and ink-stained affair—sat Inspector Vasant Kelkar. Ghote did not know him personally. But he knew of him with an intensity that well made up for the lack of personal relationship. He was to Ghote, and long had been, the star and example of all that a detective officer ought to be.

He could not remember exactly the first time he had set eyes on him, or even when he had first heard him mentioned. But he had no doubt that, whenever either event was, it had been when Inspector Kelkar was receiving congratulations on some difficult assignment brought to a triumphant conclusion. He had a mental picture of him made up of dozens of different occasions. It showed him surrounded by colleagues, their hands clapping him on the shoulder and the air round loud with cries of "Jolly good show" and "Shabash, Inspector, shabash." And Kelkar truly deserved it all. He was certainly the most efficient officer of his rank in the CID, perhaps as efficient as anyone they had ever had.

Confronted with him now, struck into dumbness, Ghote saw that his neat jowly face, above the sturdy well-kept body, had acquired at some recent time a pair of scrupulously trimmed, crisply right sideboards. Sideboards. Those emblems of all that was modern and efficient and go-ahead in life all over the globe, to judge by the pictures in the newspapers of dynamic politicians and successful men-of-ideas everywhere.

It was, in fact, something of a surprise to find Kelkar in the Bats' room at all. He had surely been due for promotion. If ever anyone was marked out for a rapid rise it was Inspector Kelkar. But no doubt this was to be his last posting in the comparatively humble rank of inspector.

The other officer seated at one of the large desks was never now likely, Ghote knew, to rise beyond inspector. Yet the coming contact with him was even more to be dreaded than the prospect of working alongside a sea-trim fighting frigate of an officer like Kelkar. Inspector Arvind Nadkarni had been his guide and mentor when he had first come into the CID.

He did not need to look across towards the big desk in the far corner of the large and airy room to know exactly how Inspector Nadkarni would look. He would be sitting crouched forward with a pair of small-lensed, gold-rimmed spectacles clamped on his nose. Through them he would be examining with patient care some document. He would be reading it to the last letter. No print had ever been so small that its import had escaped Inspector Nadkarni.

And, when the spectacles were taken off and a criminal was undergoing that quiet scrutiny, the effect would be exactly the same. No human deviousness that had not in its time yielded itself up to the prolonged, deceptively mild gaze of that old spider.

"Joining the Squad?"

It was the sharp gruffish voice of Inspector Kelkar. And with it, Ghote realised, there had gone a glance of punching suspicion.

Inwardly he quailed. What a fool he had been not to have taken every possible precaution against meeting someone as implacably efficient as Inspector Kelkar. Why, the man would see through him in seconds. Already his tone had expressed strong disbelief that this arrival on the squad was an ordinary posting.

"Yes, Inspector," he answered, rapidly as he could. "I understand it is hoped to get improved results by increasing the establishment of the squ— of the Bats."

"You understand that?" Inspector Kelkar said, cocking his neat head to one side and assuming a look of brutal penetration.

"Yes, yes," Ghote said, unable to prevent a sweat of apprehension breaking out round his neck and shoulders. "Something like that was mentioned in the memo detailing my appointment. It was a phrase only, just indicating that such was the object of my posting."

Destroy the memo. He made a mental note. He could almost see the urgent red scrawl. He must leave no clues. Just as the man he had been set to find would be destroying anything which could incriminate him. From now on he must never be other than fully on the alert.

"Hm," said Inspector Kelkar, "increase of personnel does not always equal increase of efficiency, Inspector."

His eyes dropped dismissively to the pile of First Information Reports on the glossy desktop in front of him. Within a couple of seconds he had scanned one and placed it decisively downwards at his side.

It was a respite. But Ghote knew that his troubles were only increasing. He had just had to claim that he was the sort of man who would be added to the Bats' strength in order to improve their efficiency. Would he ever be able to substantiate that? And, even if he did succeed somehow in keeping one jump ahead of Inspector Kelkar, who did not know him, there was still Inspector Nadkarni to outwit. And in his time he had made innumerable mistakes right under old Nadkarni's patient gaze.

Even now, for all that at his corner desk Nadkarni was crouching still over his papers, there could be no doubt that he had heard and had mentally docketed every word that had been spoken.

Ghote decided rapidly that attack was the best form of defence. He turned to the DSP.

"No need to introduce me to Inspector Nadkarni, sir," he said. "It was from him that I learnt all I know about CID work."

He went over to the desk in the corner and, loudly as if it had never occurred to him that Nadkarni had realised he was there at all, he said good morning.

Nadkarni looked up at him over the small, gold-rimmed lenses of his spectacles.

"Ah, Ghote," he said.

And no more.

Ghote felt words of justification come tumbling out of him.

"Yes, yes. It is me, Inspector. I am to become one of your colleagues. But— Well, you see, I did not happen to have any major inquiry on hand. So— So, you see, I was available. And here I am."

Well, he thought, at least I have told the truth. No one could call anti-pickpocketing patrol a major inquiry.

"Indeed, Inspector," Nadkarni replied, his glance returning to his work. "Well, an officer of your calibre should be a valuable addition to our strength."

What did he mean by that? Was it sarcasm? Did he suspect already that there was more to his appointment than met the eye? Or could he mean that he did think of him now as being a really useful colleague? And what reply could be offered?

Remembering at the last moment advice long ago received from Nadkarni himself, Ghote kept silent. "Sometimes no question you can think of asks as much as the question you do not put." It had been one of Nadkarni's frequently stated cautious maxims.

And it seemed to work this time as always, even on the man who had coined it. After a long silence, in which Ghote could almost feel old Nadkarni's eyes travelling patiently along the lines of the document before him, at last he looked up and spoke again.

"DSP, I would think that, subject to your approval, Inspector Ghote might be of assistance in this afternoon's affair."

For an instant or so the DSP did not answer this. His round face remained blank. But Ghote thought he knew what a debate must be going on behind the apparent placidity. Was this newcomer to be trusted with the details of whatever affair was scheduled for this afternoon? His inclination must be to say "Somebody's favourite: not an inch." But on the other hand he had been instructed to take on an additional officer. And that was as much as an order to accept him as a full member of the Squad.

Which way would it go?

"Yes," the DSP said at last. "I have no doubt Inspector Radwan could use another pair of hands, a pair of thoroughly trustworthy hands."

His soft brown eyes looked at Ghote with fumy penetration. Ghote endured them.

The DSP turned away.

"I think I can promise that your initiation into the Bats will be a good show, Inspector," he said.

Ghote stiffened his whole frame.

"I damn well hope it will be," he said.

"If," came the quiet voice of Inspector Nadkarni, crouching over his papers, "this time our smuggling friends turn up where they are expected."

Ghote, all innocent eagerness to enter the ring, was not simply five minutes early for the rendezvous he had been given with Inspector Radwan, in charge of the Bats' newest operation, he was a full ten minutes before his time. It was outside the Castle, the remains of one of Bombay's oldest buildings, now an Indian Navy establishment, that they were to meet for Ghote to receive instructions for his part in the afternoon's activities.

He stood in the post-monsoon sunshine and looked blankly at the neat gardens, the fragments of the old walls, the passing sailors in their close-fitting white uniforms with the flapping, square-cut collars and their round hats banded with the names of their ships. Beyond he saw the clock tower and recalled that he had been told the big black ball at the top fell at precisely one o'clock every day on an electric signal from Colaba Observatory.

Well, he thought, by then I shall have begun my first task with the Bats. If only it might be a success. If only it could blow away the dark clouds that Mr. Rao thinks are hanging.

He turned his mind to consider his coming meeting with Inspector Radwan. In the course of the morning, before drawing from Transport the civilian car which he had been ordered to bring to a point near the Castle for his 12:55 hours rendezvous, he had found time to inquire casually of former colleagues what they knew about this newcomer to Bombay CID. His questions had not brought him much enlightenment, and he had been afraid to press them in case people started asking why Inspector Ghote was so interested in this member of the Bats.

In the end he had to be content with learning, as was in any case evident with someone with the name of Radwan, that the newcomer was a Muslim, and that in his previous posting—one informant said it was at Ahmednagar and another at Aurangabad

—he had gained a formidable reputation for success. Such scraps were hardly enough to allow him to decide whether the fellow was likely to be a man who could sell secrets to the black-money bosses.

No, he would have to watch him with every sense alert on each and every occasion he had dealings with him. There must be something to see if the fellow was betraying them, even something as tiny as the wrong sort of look at the wrong moment, or a short unexplained absence just after new orders had been given, or perhaps some small signs of a higher rate of spending than someone on an inspector's pay should be able to manage.

And that was little enough, he reflected in a sudden access of gloom. His mind slid darkly into considering the number of pairs of trousers necessary to maintain the state of smartness appropriate to an officer working in the Bats. From there it went on to ask how many small financial requests a son of ten could reasonably be allowed. And this led, by a process that seemed entirely logical, to the details of an elaborate, shifting-round plan to reduce expenditure on food by making more use of a rather battered plantain tree that grew in the rear of his Government Quarters home. He had a great affection for this tree. He felt for it as if it was an old wheezy dog or an ancient lame horse that had belonged to the family since his childhood. Each year he cherished its few fruits as if they were great thriving stalks of the biggest bananas. He was trying to persuade himself that this would be a year when the tree would fruit really well when a tremendous buffet on the shoulder brought him crashing back to the present.

"What—" he exclaimed.

A huge laugh resounded in his ear.

He swung round. A tall man with a luxuriantly glossy beard, dressed in shirt and trousers that seemed to shine with an altogether special whiteness, was looking down at him. His eyes were sparkling with happy confidence and he was grinning widely in the entire expectation of his boisterous greeting being equally warmly returned.

"Well, well," the fellow boomed. "What a surprise to meet an old friend here of all places."

Ghote searched savagely for a retort to put the stranger thoroughly in his place. But before he had found it the fellow leant towards him and in a quick confident undertone asked: "It is Ghote?"

Radwan, Ghote realised immediately. Inspector Radwan.

Overcome with shame at having been caught daydreaming at the rendezvous hour, he glanced hastily and guiltily at his watch. But Inspector Radwan had arrived five minutes before his time.

Rapidly he admitted to being Inspector Ghote.

"They have told you nothing of this present business?" Radwan asked at once, glancing sharply at a portly matron in a deep plum-coloured sari giving two wide-eyed little girls in white frocks a loud and inaccurate history of the Castle.

"I was told only to rendezvous at 12:55 hours," Ghote said.

"Good, good," Radwan replied happily. "I insisted to have no information given out till the last moment. You have heard what happened on our last two operations?"

"Well," Ghote said with caution, "I understood they were not altogether successful."

"Not successful?" Inspector Radwan said, with abrupt and cutting bitterness. "My friend, the fact is that the men we were all ready to get just walked out of it."

His eyes, under bushy eyebrows, gleamed with ferocity.

"But this time," he said, "when it is my show, I promise you the same thing is not going to happen."

Ghote looked at him sideways. The keenly handsome face with its luxuriant beard and glossily curling moustaches under the straight prow of a nose was lit by pure passion.

Or was it playing at being lit by pure passion, Ghote asked himself. What could be a better disguise for anyone set on selling information to the black-money syndicates than crusading zeal? But then a real crusading zeal would also produce just such an effect.

No time now, however, for speculation. He tried to bring to his own eyes a zeal to match Inspector Radwan's.

"Well now," he said fierily, "what is to be my part in this?"

Low-voiced always and constantly surveying the people in this comparatively unfrequented spot just at the back of the city's huge Town Hall, Inspector Radwan outlined then the business of the afternoon.

It seemed that the remaining member of the Bats, Sub-

Inspector Patel, had learnt up in the suburb of Dadar that a large consignment of smuggled gold was about to arrive there. A powerful motor-driven dhow from Dubai in Southern Arabia would heave to off the coast and transfer the gold to a fishing boat. This would bring it to the beach somewhere in Dadar and it would at once be loaded into a car. The car would be driven into central Bombay and left in front of the Town Hall. There a new driver, already provided with the right keys, would collect it. It was expected that the car would arrive shortly after one o'clock.

There would have been a time when the police or the Customs would have been delighted simply to know in advance that a consignment of gold, probably unusually substantial after the monsoon break in smuggling, was being sent along a certain route. At whatever seemed the best point they would have swooped. And some hundred or more smugglers' pocketed jackets with each pocket containing a ten-tola gold bar bought in Dubai for, say, three hundred American dollars, would be seized. There would have been a great deal of congratulation all round.

But the Bats were after bigger prey than this. They needed to get at the men financing with that powerful untraceable black money dozens or even hundreds of deals like this. The black-money seths, Radwan called them with an edge of anger in his voice. Real anger or feigned?

So two ordinary-looking cars were due soon to arrive outside the great long colonnade of the Town Hall looking out at Horniman Circle with its seven converging roads leading into the wide circular street surrounding the inner garden, an ideal place for smugglers apprehensive of pursuit. One of the cars would be driven by Inspector Kelkar and the other by Inspector Nadkarni. Together, by means of a radio link which was all that distinguished them from the thousands of other cars tangling up Bombay, they intended to follow the smugglers' vehicle. And whatever location was being used to distribute the big new supply of gold they ought, if all went well, to be able to get on to a seth as yet untouched.

With two cars alternating in the chase the driver of the vehicle with the gold ought not, however anxiously alert he was, to have any suspicions that he was under observation. But it was always possible that in the busy afternoon traffic both pursuers might lose the quarry. So Ghote, in yet a third radio-linked car, would be a useful addition to the team.

"You think you could do it, keep up with this fellow?" Inspector Radwan asked finally, looking down at Ghote from his full six feet of height.

Suspecting a trace of contempt, Ghote was about to retort that of course he could do something as simple. But, mercifully, better sense prevailed.

"What type of vehicle is this smugglers' car?" he asked. "Do we know that?"

"It is American, perhaps a Chrysler," Radwan answered.

Ghote thought he detected the almost imperceptible erasure of the contempt.

"It is new or old?" he asked, pressing home his point.

"Not very old. Patel was not certain of anything but the vehicle's number."

Ghote sighed.

"Well, I was given by Transport a Standard only," he said. "So, you know, if it is a question of following outside the city, I would not be able to hold a car like that for ten minutes."

"Nothing to worry, nothing to worry," Radwan answered, with white teeth gleaming in the depths of his black beard. "These fellows have to use a flat somewhere in the city. The carriers who take a thousand tolas each would arouse suspicion anywhere outside. You know what country people are."

"Then," Ghote said with decision, "I shall be able to follow."

"Very good," Radwan said. "Then you had better take up station now. Keep driving round the Circle till you spot the fellow."

Ghote turned to go. Radwan gave him another hearty slap on the back, as if one old friend was parting from another accidentally encountered. Ghote wished the simulation had not involved quite so much physical force.

Behind the Muslim's broad frame, with startling suddenness, the time-signal ball in the clock tower dropped plummeting down. One o'clock exactly.

To Ghote the signal seemed the sharp clang of the boxer's bell at the start of Round 1. There was a black-money seth to be outfought: he would punch with the best of them. And, although he did recall that he was meant to be fighting not a seth but some unknown one among his own new colleagues, he found it hard to summon up any antagonism other than towards the just-coming-into-range evildoer. The adversary with power to cripple him in a way he had not at that moment the least notion of was to him still totally invisible.

IV

It was seventeen minutes past one by the clock in the tower of the Anglican Cathedral overlooking Horniman Circle when Ghote, driving sedately round in his little Standard, spotted a big green Chrysler coming into the traffic stream from the direction of Flora Fountain, the most likely route for a vehicle from Dadar. It was a good way ahead of him and he was unable to see its number plate. But American cars were not common among the mass of home-produced Ambassadors, Fiats, and Standards and he felt this was quite likely to be the expected smugglers' vehicle.

He pictured to himself its rear floor where the gold-carrying jackets would be piled hidden under a rug or an old piece of gunny. A hundred jackets, each with a hundred little pockets sewn up in its strong canvas. And in each pocket a flat bar of dully glinting metal, something over two inches long, something over an inch wide, thick only as a slab of chocolate. And each one would be identical: stamped with the name of a Swiss bank, with the words 10 TOLAS and with the figures 999.0, pure gold as near as could be got, secretly gleaming with its unique, infinitely yearned for presence.

Glancing at the traffic to either side, he urged the chugging little Standard forward. First check that number, then be ready to park when the period for the exchange of smugglers' drivers began.

Had Kelkar and Nadkarni also seen the Chrysler?

But at the thought of the two of them the excitement of the encounter with the gold-carrying car drained sharply away. Ghote's stomach experienced a sudden sick constriction. Could it be possible that one of those two had already contrived to send a message to whatever seth was running this operation? Was the figure at the end of their trail already warned that an attempt was being made to trace the gold to him? Was patient, crouching Nadkarni or Kelkar, that thrusting fighting frigate, sitting at the wheel at this moment plotting how best to lose the Chrysler as they tracked it? And gloating over the fat sum to come for doing it?

It must not be.

And it need not be. There was Inspector Radwan. As organiser of the present operation he was in a better position than anybody to inform the seth of what was planned. What to think of Inspector Radwan?

Pushing through the cars and the taxis, the trucks and the big goods lorries, the buses and the everywhere skitter of bicycles, Ghote tried in vain to find some significant clue in his encounter with the Muslim. The fellow had shown himself certainly to be very zealous. But confidence of that sort could take a person as far along the path leading to the large and surreptitious black-money handout as along that leading to the tracking down of the offender.

And he must not let himself be influenced by the fact that he did not somehow care for breezy Inspector Radwan.

Or there was still Sub-Inspector Patel. With a name like that he could be one of a dozen or twenty officers in the State force. What would he turn out to be like? Or there was DSP Naik. But here was a thought that brought everything to a stop.

The unseen adversary had loosed a first jab.

Ah, it looked as if the Chrysler had found a space to park right in front of the great descent of steps from the Town Hall. In a few moments he would pass the spot and then—

Hell.

Ghote felt himself go suddenly hot with embarrassment. The Chrysler was not the right car. Its number, coming abruptly into view, was not the MHB 1255 that Inspector Radwan had given him but MHB 2255.

Waves of doubt crashed up onto the beach of his mind. Could Inspector Radwan have got the number wrong? It seemed an extraordinary coincidence that two cars with such similar numbers were both going to turn up in the one place at the same time. Yet even from his short talk with the Muslim it was plain he was not the sort to make mistakes. He exuded confidence in the rightness of everything he said and did. And he had even repeated the number.

Ghote longed to use his radio. A check with either of those pillars of reliability, Nadkarni or Kelkar, would quell at once this storm of doubt. But total radio silence had been imposed until after the smugglers' car had started on its second journey, and even then only the most brief and necessary messages were to be passed. He could not, a one-day recruit to the Bats, defy orders at the very start.

Miserable and alone, he drove once more round the Circle. The calm green of the gardens inside slowly changed its pattern while the bucketing competing traffic beyond sent its noise and its fumes quivering into the steamy end-of-monsoon air.

But when he arrived at the low, calmly impressive, colonnaded bulk of the Town Hall once again—he had hoped that mysteriously the Chrysler's number would now after all be MHB 1255—he saw parked only half a dozen spaces from the vehicle a well-kept Ambassador with crouching over its wheel Inspector Nadkarni. He felt reassurance seeping rapidly back into him like water into a dried gourd skin.

Even from a passing glimpse it was possible to feel the patience radiating from old Nadkarni. And, whatever the significance of the one-digit difference in the Chrysler's number, patient Nadkarni was plainly unperturbed by it. He would be sitting there calmly assessing the probabilities. He would be waiting simply to see which way the cat jumped. And when it did he would have plans ready. Whichever way it jumped. Or however many cats there were.

There was a parking space vacant just off the Circle in Mint Road, opposite the big blank concrete structure of the Reserve Bank of India. Ghote decided to grab it. He manoeuvred the Standard round till he had it facing the whirligig of the Circle. From where he eventually came to rest he could just glimpse the Chrysler in front of the Town Hall steps.

What would happen now? Would a second big American car really arrive on the scene? Perhaps though it had been Sub-Inspector Patel who had got the number wrong. Yet would a man like Radwan have allowed him to slip up like that? No, never in a hundred years. So a second MHB car must soon appear.

Ah, there was Inspector Kelkar, also in an Ambassador.

Ghote watched as he passed the parked Chrysler and went on

around the Circle out of sight. He had not moved his neat, long-sideboarded head by so much as half an inch. But it could not be doubted that he had seen the vehicle. And its number. What action would he take?

Ghote felt the sticky sweat that the situation had brought up all over his body positively drying away at the thought of Kelkar's presence. That man was a solid-grained black rock. Let the seas foam.

Ten minutes passed. Inspector Kelkar did not come into view again, and Ghote decided that he must too have parked.

Cars slid by him making their way into the Circle. On the pavement on the other side pedestrians moved this way and that in shifting blocks. People of every nationality under the sun, brought to Bombay and its commercial heart. Indians from every state of the union, Marathis like himself, Gujeratis, bold-featured and fleshy, now a Pathan watchman, striding by as if the flat heat-soaked paving stones were a hill path, in his stiff yellow turban and wide white and dirty trousers. And beyond him someone from the far eastern borders, flat-faced and slant-eyed and short of stature. And there were smartly dressed Japanese, as well as Europeans by the dozen, most of them wedded to neckties and jackets, almost every one of them clutching a brief case. What nationalities would they be? Americans and Englishmen were easy enough to spot. But what about that chap who looked a little like a Goan, would he be Portuguese? Perhaps.

A shaikh in flowing Arab robes got out of an air-cooled limousine and a beggar, shuffling by on the kerb edge between the hurrying businessmen and the parked cars, looked in through the window of his own vehicle. A slime-streaked face.

But Ghote hardly saw him. Down in the Circle the head of a man had appeared just on the far side of the parked Chrysler. He looked as if he was a Sikh, to judge by the neat blue turban and the glimpse of a beard. In a moment he ducked down. He must be getting into the car.

Was this simply the innocent vehicle's owner returning to it? There had been no chance of seeing him as he had left. The time that they had expected the gold-carrying car to come had passed, but it still could arrive.

If only the radio was not banned.

Ghote felt swarms of possibilities begin to race in his mind. He made a mental grab to gain at least some stability. He would trust Inspector Radwan. A man of that much assurance was not going to be wrong. He would sit tight here until he saw the proper smugglers' car, MHB 1255.

He watched with enormous calm the Chrysler nose out into the traffic going round the Circle. It turned in his direction. Deliberately he forced himself to look beyond it. After all, the parking space it had abandoned would make an excellent place for the real smugglers' car. There were not so many spaces now, and the fellow coming was behind his time.

When the Chrysler actually went past him he was concentrating so hard on cars approaching the vacant parking space that he hardly noticed it. But then, upsetting his precariously fixed world in an instant, his eye caught, coming towards him along Mint Road, an Ambassador with a distinctly familiar driver. Crouching, spiderlike, over the wheel was Inspector Nadkarni.

So, he thought in a whirl, the smugglers' car must be MHB 2255 after all. Inspector Nadkarni, the soul of thoroughness, was not going to make a mistake over a thing like a car number.

And, in immediate confirmation of this judgment, a second Ambassador, Inspector Kelkar's, came into Mint Road.

Kelkar was moving fast, out towards the middle of the road. He was slipping his way past cars and lorries in a manner that would have done credit to the most thrusting of Sikh taxi drivers. It was obvious that the tactics were going to be for him to take station ahead of the Chrysler. Then, when he did drop back and follow, the smugglers' driver would have no doubts.

Ghote started up his own engine, which he had thought better to leave to cool while he was parked. To his relief it did not fail. He waited for a chance to slip out into the traffic and take up his position as third man in the chase. He switched on the radio. Now he was in touch again, though he doubted if much would be said over the open air. Nadkarni and Kelkar were altogether too old hands at this game to need to communicate except in a crisis.

He had to wait however for a considerable period before he could cut across the traffic and swing northwards. By the time the little chugging Standard was on its way he could no longer see either of his fellow hunters' Ambassadors. But with the radio's on-light glinting down below the dashboard he was not worried. He went as far as the huge mass of the GPO, from which there were as many as nine different routes a car coming from Mint Road could take. And there he pulled in to the kerb and waited.

The pigeons on the swinging lines of the telephone wires leading from the great domed GPO building barged and shuffled for position. Occasionally one came down in a beating flutter of grey wings to where it had spotted some possibly edible morsel.

Ghote, feeling now quite suddenly soothed, was happy to watch them. He was embarked on the simple pursuit. All he had to do at this moment was to wait for directions and then follow them up as hard as he could go. Later he could try to work out what everything that had happened meant. If that should prove necessary. Later he might have to ask if some particular action had indicated that Inspector Nadkarni had, impossibly, behaved a little out of character. Later he might have to wonder whether after all Inspector Kelkar had been less than superbly efficient. Now he did not have to worry.

And in the dark his simple zest added all the more surely to the strength of his real antagonist dancing hoveringly just within striking distance.

Then at last directions. A brief crackle from the radio. Then the swift, semi-coded message.

"Green here. Monkey has taken First Marine Street."

Green meant Inspector Nadkarni and Monkey was the name given to the smugglers' car. Immediately Ghote brought to his mind's eye a sketch map of all the crisscrossing streets in this hub of Bombay. First Marine Street, of course, led from the north corner of the Azad Maidan, that urchin cricketers' nursery, across westwards to the long north-and-south run of Queen's Road.

All he had to do was to work himself round to the left and enter Cruickshank Road at the east corner of the triangular maidan. He was not far behind in the chase.

Now, as the Standard began to chug up Cruickshank Road, there came Inspector Kelkar's voice on the radio, chopped and quick.

"White here. Wrong-footed. Am taking Princess Street however and will pick up there."

Again Ghote saw the situation laid out map-like. Princess Street ran parallel to First Marine Street three hundred yards or so farther north. Kelkar, ahead of the smugglers' car, though caught out by its sharp turn-off, was not out of the game. Almost certainly the Chrysler would turn north at Queen's Road. That way lay all the alternative hiding places that the northern part of the city offered. And, if the smugglers' driver went north, Kelkar could easily pick him up as he came past the junction of Queen's Road and Princess Street. Nor would he at all suspect a car taking the same route from that point only.

Hugging the Standard's wheel, Ghote urged the sluggish little vehicle onwards.

And then trouble came. First Nadkarni's voice, still patient but urgent enough.

"We are putting on speed. Hurry White."

And then Kelkar. Plainly furious.

"Bloody breakdown ahead. No way through. Keep with him Green."

So the plan to nip in behind the Chrysler at the junction was out. It was up to Inspector Nadkarni now.

And to me, Ghote added, in mixed apprehension and excitement.

He finished his run up alongside the tree-surrounded Azad Maidan and prepared to turn into First Marine Street. He could feel the engine in front of him throbbing in a distinctly ominous way. There was even less speed in the little car than he had counted on.

And now worse trouble. Nadkarni's voice, sounding clearly resigned.

"Green. Monkey is going at a first-class lick. I am losing him."

Ghote felt a well-up of disappointment. The chase, which had seemed so promising, was petering out already. If Nadkarni in an Ambassador was being outpaced, there was no hope for himself in a Standard and already farther behind.

But then the radio crackled into life again.

"White to Saffron. I suspect Monkey was ready for a chase. So if he is going hard north now it is possible his eventual destination is really south. Can you get across to Marine Drive to intercept? Over."

Ghote licked quickly at his lips. He was Saffron, the third colour of the Indian flag reading downwards. And he saw at once what Saffron's task was now to be. Marine Drive exactly paralleled Queen's Road, running north and south, but right next to the sea. If Monkey really did intend to throw off pursuit by going hard north and then doubling back southwards, it was a good gamble that he would take Marine Drive to do this. So if this little choked-up monster of a vehicle could be got across to the big south-going sweep in time he could pick up the trail again. The only difficulty was that there was no direct road across. Between Queen's Road, which he was now approaching, and Marine Drive only some two hundred and fifty yards farther west there lay the railway line from Churchgate Station with neither bridge nor tunnel to cross it.

Getting to a point where he could intercept Monkey meant going south down Queen's Road for a good mile until he hit Marine Drive. What with the traffic and the Standard's choking engine it would not be easy to get there in time.

He picked up the radio microphone.

"Saffron," he said. "Will do."

Negotiating the turn out into Queen's Road, he felt a small glow of pride. His response to Inspector Kelkar's call had surely been precise and laconic enough to have come from the lips of that great man himself.

Past the hospital on the left with the unending stretch of Lloyd Recreation Ground, green and open, on the right. The damned engine seemed to be going a bit better now. All-India Radio on the left. Good. And the Income-tax Office. Must pay that soon. What a drain. And to think of all those black-money boys escaping it. The Tourist Office now. He would do it. He would do it.

Now Churchgate Station on the left and that great pile of the Western Railway offices on the right. A hell of a lot of traffic to turn into in Vir Nariman Road. But the light's changing . . . If I get through on the tail of this lot . . .

Yes. Yes. Yes. Swinging round with the last of them. And there in the distance ahead the shine of the sea. How far along to Marine Drive? A quarter of a mile? Perhaps a bit more. Western India AAA offices. The Tea Centre. That hotel. Never remember which. Past it now. All those travel agencies on the left in front of the Brabourne Stadium. Test Cricket. What would it be like having enough money to fly away for holi—

Right. Right. Here we are. Just in here. First-class view all the way up along Marine Drive. See that Chrysler easily. Wonderful.

Should he tell them on the radio? Just a simple "Saffron in position"? No. No, it was not necessary. Inspector Kelkar would never waste words like that. No, just wait. Be like old Nadkarni and wait in patience.

After all, it was a big gamble that the Chrysler would come back this way at all. A brilliant stroke on the part of Inspector Kelkar if his guess proved right. But a mere waste of time if the gold was taken, as it well could be, to some destination in the northern suburbs as far as could be from this southern tip of the sea-surrounded city.

In front, beyond the broad stretch of the sweeping road and the line of shrubs that split it into two, the sea lay, grey-blue and uneasy. Dark rain clouds had gathered to the north behind the high jutting outline of Malabar Point. No doubt a heavy shower was beating down somewhere out in the ocean. Perhaps it would swing in and give the steamy city a welcome drenching.

Steadily Ghote watched the stream of cars coming down on his right. Plenty of time to act as soon as he spotted the green colour of the Chrysler. Plenty of time to ease into the crossing traffic stream after it had passed, its driver happily convinced that he had thrown off all pursuit. Then it would be a matter of sitting, like an unobtrusive beetle, just behind and of following to whatever final destination it led.

Then, bowling along easily behind a black Fiat, there it was. Unmistakable long before it was possible to make out that MHB 2255 number plate, the Chrysler.

Inspector Ghote smiled comfortably. And then the dark adversary struck out once. Was he after all, he thought suddenly, actually meant to be there? Was he meant to be overconfidently expecting to track that car down?

Was somebody very clever, he asked himself, relying on this not particularly successful inspector in his wheezing little Standard to lose the quarry after all? To lose it in such a way that no one could be blamed for a failure that had really been deliberately contrived? No one but that unsuccessful inspector?

V

The thought of what had perhaps been done to him almost froze Ghote into inactivity at the very moment that he should have urged his chugging Standard out into the traffic in the wake of the comfortably cruising gold-laden Chrysler. Almost but not completely. The plan of action, which he had run through in his head a dozen times or more as he had sat waiting for the Chrysler to come, saw him mechanically through the crisis.

He succeeded in taking up a place just in the rear of that familiar number plate MHB 2255. Without difficulty he accommodated his speed to that of his quarry.

But his mind was in turmoil. With the fight hardly begun suddenly he was on the ropes dazedly taking a battering.

What if, he kept saying, he was at this moment simply acting out a part in a cunning scheme devised by whoever was betraying the Bats? Say it was Inspector Kelkar. It would have been easily possible for him to pretend to get caught in some imaginary traffic holdup and so not be able to pick up the trail of the speeding Chrysler. But to have done that would have left him not beyond the reach of suspicion. So had he cunningly sent that radio appeal to Saffron, confident that Saffron would never be able to tail the Chrysler to its final destination?

He could have planned it. Or Inspector Nadkarni could have taken advantage of a guiltless Kelkar's suggestion, certain that this new recruit to the Bats whom he knew so well would never be able to do what was asked of him. Or even Inspector Radwan, that dazzling Moslem, could have during their brief meeting rapidly assessed his potential and have confidently allowed him to walk into what he would think of as certain failure. Or the DSP himself? But that was too terrible to contemplate.

But what was abundantly clear was that he might well now be being left to make a mess of the whole of the operation.

Well, he would not. Whatever might happen, he would not. With simple resolution he turned to fight the enemy he could see.

The traffic, as the Chrysler turned left off the wide boulevard into D'Watcha Road, was quite heavy enough to prevent the big car using its speed to get away from him. So he would sit on its tail, twist and cheat how it might, till at last it reached its destination.

Tensely he hunched over the Standard's wheel, coaxing the thick engine to its best performance. Constantly he glanced to this side and that to assess the intentions of every scooter driver, of every cyclist. He was going to make sure no one got between him and his man.

At the end of the short run of D'Watcha Road, coming into Queen's Road again just opposite the tall Rajabi Tower on the far side of the open space of the Oval, the Chrysler turned right, heading southwards towards the very tip of the sea-jutting city, Colaba.

Well, there would be side turnings enough in that crowded area of old houses, built round courtyards and jam-packed with people. Between the old brown-coloured stone buildings, split into hundreds of modest flats, once in sight of the blessed cooling sea, now mostly cut off from it by the towering new white buildings of the reclamation land, there would be opportunities in plenty for a car suddenly to vanish. Plenty of chances for a driver suspecting he was being followed to take a sharp turn.

But it was also an ever-narrowing promontory, never more than half a mile across. So if a vehicle did succeed in throwing off its pursuer, there was plenty of chance of that pursuer finding its quarry again.

Down towards it all they went, between the football Mecca of the Cooperage and the more select areas of the Ladies Gymkhana and the Commercial Gymkhana. And Ghote kept the wheezing Standard always within a car's length of the Chrysler, every moment flickeringly alert.

Into Wodehouse Road they came with its big houses set in substantial gardens and ornate with heavy balconies. And still the blue-turbaned Sikh in the Chrysler seemed unconscious of any pursuit. And still Ghote hung on to his tail, feeling the heat from the Standard's engine, already driven too rigorously too long, sweeping up at him in a sharp belt of churned air.

Had the fellow really not noticed this car that had taken the same route and kept so closely behind all the way now from the end of Marine Drive? Perhaps not. It was a route that a fair amount of traffic might reasonably follow.

And then, abruptly, the Chrysler turned off to the left.

Ghote sat half an inch farther forward on the old chafed seat of the Standard. From now on the opportunities for the sharp twist away down a side turning would really begin.

Almost at once the first of them came. But he managed to stay in the wake of the Chrysler without difficulty.

Well, it could not be many minutes now before that Sikh registered that a certain little Standard had been following precisely his own zigzag route.

Ghote licked at his lips.

Another sharp turn. An old victoria, drawn by a lean bone-jutting horse, pulled out of the side street immediately after the Chrysler had slipped into it. Ghote, swinging round in his turn, had to tread hard on his brakes. The Standard's much-coaxed engine stalled. The victoria crept along.

And the Chrysler was nowhere to be seen.

With sweat-slippery fingers Ghote got his engine going again and went charging down the side street to the danger of all the half-dozen pi-dogs ranging about in it.

But he hit none of them. And, even when a swollen-belly, flap-eared cow at the far end lurched into his path as he came up in a choked roar of sound, he contrived to swerve past. With clouds of blue exhaust billowing out behind, he took the turning at the far end.

And then, again, he had to brake hard. The Chrysler had come to a halt not fifty yards along the road.

The street into which they had come was a moderately prosperous one of tall brown-coloured buildings, six storeys high and divided into flats. The Chrysler was parked between two of them.

So which one was the place where the smuggled gold was going to be distributed, Ghote asked himself. He let the Standard's engine die into silence and began to study the surroundings.

The street was busy. People were going in and out of the tall brown buildings. Ghote put them down as being on the whole somewhat unrespectable. They would be journalists, musicians, actors and actresses, film types, some perhaps still hoping to make star status and move up to the big apartments on Malabar Hill and others who had resigned themselves to never achieving that dazzling success but who still clung to its glamour.

Ghote watched them all like a tiger.

The Sikh had not got out of the Chrysler. His blue turban was clearly visible through the rear window. Was he even now looking in the mirror and asking himself, in a hot twitch of suspicion, why that Standard he had seen so often was parked just behind him?

Ghote's hand stole to the starting button on the dashboard. If the fellow was to drive off suddenly he must be ready.

But the Sikh showed no sign of departing. Evidently he must be waiting for someone to come down from whatever flat had been temporarily rented as a distribution point for the gold. And he would have to stay with the car. Its load was far too valuable to leave hereabouts, even locked up. Merely to carry all those pocketed jackets up to the flat would be a considerable task for one man. The hundred ten-tola bars in each one of them must weigh something like twenty-five pounds.

Yet, when, after a wait of some five minutes, someone did go up to the Sikh as he sat smoking a cigarette Ghote was caught completely on the hop by them.

It was a woman.

Aware of the need to guard the precious contents of the car, and of the effort required to get them up the stairs of whichever building was being used, Ghote had discounted the women he had seen coming out of either of the two entrances that he was keeping a special watch on. So before he was much conscious of her, the prettyish creature in her early thirties, wearing a deep red sari with a bold blue border, was already leaning in at the Chrysler's window talking animatedly to the Sikh. She might have come out of either building, or from none at all.

All right, he said to himself sharply, and why should one of the gold-smuggling gang not be a woman? I must altogether throw out these innocent tendencies of mine.

He watched her as she went on speaking to the Sikh. No doubt in a moment she would slip into the car and guard it while the Sikh began carrying up the jackets.

But, to his slight surprise, after half a minute more the woman backed away from the Chrysler's window. She was smiling largely and saying something he was much too far way to have any chance of hearing. And then she turned and came along the narrow pavement in his direction.

He felt vague suspicions stirring inside him, like so many scorpions waking when heat struck them. Who was this person? Why had she talked to the Sikh if she was not going to get into the car? Where was she going now? What had she said to the Sikh?

Jab, jab, jab went the real adversary. And Ghote was blissfully unaware he had suffered the least damage.

He snatched up the Standard's logbook and pretended to be consulting it, as if he were a salesman with a list of addresses to go to. And out of the corner of his eye he watched the woman as she came towards him.

There seemed, as far as he could see, to be nothing particularly suspicious about her. She was, he confirmed, decidedly attractive. She had a full fresh face which the sharply implanted red kumkum on her forehead set off splendidly. Though full figured, she moved with grace.

She got nearer and nearer and he continued to examine her, his head bent still over the logbook. What could she have wanted with the Sikh? And why had she left him and come in this direc—

Suddenly her face appeared at the window beside him and he saw her fingers tapping on the thick glass. She was smiling broadly, telegraphing him a message of reassurance. Yet he felt his heart beginning to beat fast in half-frightened perplexity.

Was she some sort of prostitute? His mind stretched out this way and that for fresh suspicions. But, though he could think of no other explanation for her conduct, his supposition seemed on the face of it quite unlikely.

He made himself wind down the window.

"Please, could you help?"

She giggled. She was really very attractive. Not with his wife's clear-cut elegance. But with a chubby and obvious sweetness that was like a big purple ice cream.

"You will think me crazy," she said. "But I am lost."

"Lost?"

"Yes. You see, I was visiting friends somewhere back there, and I left my car on Wodehouse Road. Well, I found the place all right when I was coming. But now I cannot find my way to Wodehouse Road again, and I cannot find where I have come from."

Ghote looked at her. To be so stupid: it gave her an extra attractiveness. A rarity value.

He was not sorry when abruptly she tugged at the door in front of her, apparently believing she would be able to speak more easily through a whole opened door than merely through the wound-down window.

"It really is not very difficult to get to Wodehouse Road from here," he said.

"Oh. Oh. Marvellous. Fantastic. Truly."

"Fantastic" was something of a craze word in film circles, Ghote reflected. Or so it seemed from his occasional, rather shame-faced reading of film-gossip magazines. So the lost lady was most probably an actress visiting friends in the profession here. The encounter would make an interesting story to tell Protima when he got home.

But would Protima be jealous? His common sense reassured him.

The first swift uppercut to the solar plexus, ignored completely.

The actress was prattling on.

"I knew when I spotted you that you were the reliable type. I mean, I asked a Sikh back there. I mean, they're supposed to be so mechanically minded and everything. And all he did was to get me in a hopeless muddle. But I think you must be different. Definitely."

She thrust herself even more into the car.

Good gracious, Ghote thought, does she really think it is necessary to do all this to me just to get directions only?

He decided he had better tell her what she needed to know as quickly as possible.

"Listen, it is very simple," he said. "You cross this road. And then you take any one of the turnings off it. And you go—"

"No, no, no."

Ghote stopped and stared at her. What could she mean?

She giggled.

"But you must not do that to me," she said.

"Not to do what?"

"Not tell me to take any road. You see, I have no road sense. No road sense at all. East is east and west is west to me. Or do I mean the other way round?"

Ghote blinked.

"Yes," he said, "I think if you mean that you have no road sense you do mean the other way—"

She was commanding all his interest. Her face was close to his. He was headily aware of the cleanly attractive odour of the best paan on her breath and of the scent of attar of roses. But a tiny corner of his attention had nevertheless been given all along to the Sikh in the parked Chrysler. And the Sikh was suddenly driving off.

"Excuse me," Ghote shouted.

He swung away to the wheel. Damn it. Why had he let the engine stop? He started it again. Savagely.

And the damn silly girl was still leaning in at the open door. Stupid, stupid creature.

"Get out. I must go."

"No, but you see no road sense. No road—"

He turned aside momentarily and gave her a sharp push. The Chrysler was gathering speed fast. In a moment it would reach a turning, take it and be lost.

"Oh, oh, playful mister," the stupid girl said.

She gave Ghote a push in her turn.

Leaving regrets for afterwards, Ghote swung fully towards her, seized her by both her wrists, leant backwards a little and then brought his whole body forwards in one sharp jerk. The girl flew out of the car and sat down on the pavement.

Without waiting to close the wide-flapping door, Ghote sent his little vehicle shooting out into the roadway. It was only as he corrected violently to avoid a waterseller's handcart that he realised that the actress-girl had been doing nothing else but make it possible for the smugglers' car to get clear.

By the time he reached the corner it had, of course, completely disappeared.

The inquiry into the loss of the gold-smugglers' car in DSP Naik's office later that afternoon was sombre. The DSP, his round face like a glum moon, summed up after he had heard their reports.

"There can be no doubt about it," he said. "Someone told those people just what Ghote here looked like and what car he would be driving. It was just bloody sharp work on their part to use that actress-woman to warn the Sikh and then hold you up like that, Ghote."

"Yes, sir," Ghote said lumpily.

He lacked the force to add a single word to that. The very thought of the "actress" sent fog rolls of gloom pouring on him.

But Inspector Radwan, sitting upright and glossy-bearded with his chair drawn well up to the DSP's desk, did have a comment.

"Ah, what is there to be depressed, Inspector Ghote? No one can blame you for falling for a pretty girl."

Ghote turned a stiff-faced look on him.

"That is," Radwan added sharply, "if you did fall."

"If he did fall?" the DSP said. "What do you mean, Inspector?"

"Sir," Ghote answered, his awareness sharpened to fever-point by the thousand suspicions that had tumbled through his mind ever since the abortive chase had come to its end. "Sir, Inspector Radwan is questioning if I allowed that Sikh to get away on purpose."

"But that is non—"

And the DSP stopped. It was horribly easy to see him thinking that what Inspector Radwan had said might not after all be such nonsense.

Inspector Nadkarni coughed dryly behind his hand, his customary signal that he had something to say.

"I think, DSP, you are quite right: we can dismiss the thought of Ghote being deliberately the cause of the trouble. Until yesterday he was on anti-pickpocketing duties only."

Ghote felt a surge of gratitude. But it was swamped even as it invaded him. The thought that, whatever his own position, the man responsible for their whole operation failing was in all probability sitting in the room with them now loomed over everything like a Himalayan glacier.

Was it possible that the man was the DSP himself? Was it Radwan? And, for all that jibe about him deliberately letting that "actress" delay him, he did not even want it to be the Muslim. So was it Nadkarni? Or Kelkar? That it should be either seemed to him worse even than that it should be the DSP. Or was it, in a different way as bad again, young Sub-Inspector Patel?

Because this Patel was the last among all the Patels in the whole State force that he had expected to find as a member of the Bats. He had been at Police Training College with him. Dayabhai Patel was somewhat younger than himself in age and back at the college had seemed at least a decade younger in experience. But despite this they had been close friends, and he had as much as he could protected the lad. And he had certainly needed protection. He had been, of all the green detective trainees assembled up at Nasik, the most gawpingly innocent. When coarse practical jokes had been played Dayabhai was always the first butt of them. At last even the most unwearying jokers had tired of him, and had generally turned their attention to his friend. But he himself had soon enough learnt how to cope with such people: Dayabhai never had.

He had got through the course, just. But everybody had been convinced that he was destined for a career strictly in the lower ranks of the CID. He might, they said, rise to Sergeant, because he was intelligent enough. But beyond that he would never go.

But now here he was, Sub-Inspector Patel.

Ghote looked at him. He was much as he had always been, incurably young-looking despite the moustache he had acquired and a few more wrinkles and roughnesses on the face. Whatever changes time had brought, he had not lost the curious trick he had had of constantly craning his neck forwards and upwards like a goose peering at something it cannot quite make out. And, although he was now wearing a neat white shirt and a well-pressed pair of brown cotton trousers, he still contrived, as he had done in uniform at Nasik, to make his garments look always a little too small for him. There was, now as of old, too much ankle and too much wrist.

In a brief talk just before the DSP's meeting, Ghote had learnt that it was due to Inspector Radwan that Dayabhai had come to Bombay. Radwan had been imported to the Bats because, coming from outside the city CID he would not be tainted by possible connections with the Bombay underworld. And, once he had arrived, he had earnestly recommended his previous sergeant. So Dayabhai, promoted as Sub-Inspector Patel, had joined the Bats and had just had his first triumph out among the fishing community at Dadar—only to have that success, thanks to the wiles of that "actress," run hopelessly away into the sand.

Yet could Dayabhai in fact be the traitor in the Bats' camp? Was it possible, if he was as simple as of old, that he had already become entangled with some badmash or other? And that they were putting the pressure on?

But Ghote was saved from exploring the full implications of such thoughts any further. Inspector Kelkar had a contribution to make to the discussion.

"DSP," he said sharply, "what we have to do now, it is plain, is to concentrate on how those fellows got to know what radio frequency we were using. Someone in their hideout must have heard my call to Ghote when I was stuck behind that breakdown in Princess Street."

Ghote experienced a quick dart of shame at this. One of the first things he had done on getting back to the office was to make a quick discreet inquiry of an acquaintance in Traffic Branch. And there had really been a major holdup in Princess Street at 1:30 pip emma.

But Kelkar had not finished.

"I have been giving the matter some thought, DSP. And I have found a breach in our security. Transport. They knew down there that our three cars had been specially requisitioned for the Bats' use. It would not have been too difficult for someone to have passed on the radio frequency set for them."

Trust Inspector Kelkar to force his way to the break in the chain of logic, Ghote thought. And, for this once at least, it meant that the betrayer was not necessarily one of the Bats. If only he himself could also batter his way to seeing similar flaws in the other two affairs. If only he could prove that the rotten apple was not one of themselves.

The unseen antagonist feinted neatly.

But Inspector Kelkar had by no means yet shown the full extent of his capabilities. Hardly had the DSP agreed that in future the Bats would have to take charge of all their own transport arrangements when Kelkar thrust his neat sideboarded head forward with another suggestion.

"Listen," he said, "so far we have let the opposition make all the running. Waiting to hear of smuggling attempts and then trying to make use of them is all very well, but something much better is needed."

Ghote leant a little farther back in his chair at the edge of the semicircle drawn up in front of the DSP's desk. He wanted to be able to look steadily at this man, to draw from the very sight of him something of that splendid fighting spirit.

Yet, he noted, really he was not all that extraordinary to look at. True, hardly any police officers had been daring enough so far to adopt those sideboards. But otherwise Kelkar's scrupulously clean-shaven face and his crisply barbered hair, even the jutting angle of his jaw, could be paralleled a score of times among the better CID officers. But there was something else in the man that could be found in only one person in ten thousand: that never-failing response of hitting back whatever the circumstances. No wonder Kelkar had risen so fast in the service. No wonder that everyone knew that another promotion was due for him. Indeed, overdue.

Promotion overdue? The idea reared up in Ghote's head like a cobra. Could it be that all that magnificent spirit had turned sour? Was it being, even as it put forward this new plan, merely superbly active in issuing a smoke screen to hide its own betrayal of everything that should be sacred?

He listened to the unfolding of the details of Kelkar's plan with twangingly strung intensity. Could he catch in them some tiny falseness, some little clue to something that was not what it seemed? Could he catch this even in Inspector Kelkar?

"I have been thinking of every possible contact point with black money," Kelkar went on. "And it seems to me that the place where we could get our hands on to what is happening without having to wait for the seths to make a move first is the foreign-exchange racket with the people who have relatives working in the UK."

Ghote, despite the closeness with which he was trying to analyse every tiniest variation of expression on those neat and pugnacious features, could not but admire the precision of Inspector Kelkar. He had hit on this field of inquiry with the accuracy of a rifle marksman. The contribution to black-money deals made by the cash sent from England by workers who had migrated there was well known. A man earning the enormous sums factory work brought there could make substantial payments to relatives at home. He should send these through the official channels at the official rates of exchange. He seldom did. And it was easy to see why: black-money syndicates would pay as much as 50 or even 60 per cent above the official rate of exchange for money put into their pools abroad. The sums, multiplied many hundreds of times when all the contributors were taken into account, would be used to buy gold, or nylon yarn or the watches that people in India so much liked. And the proceeds of the sales when the goods had been smuggled in would easily finance the payments to the relatives in India.

And—here was the beauty of Inspector Kelkar's idea—those relatives appeared like so many tiny lengths of cotton lying loose on top of the dense fabric of deceit. Gently tweak at enough of them and you would almost certainly find one that would lead back, tweak by tweak, through sub-agents and agents, to one of the seths.

"And then we go in," Inspector Kelkar said, neatly concluding Ghote's train of thought. "We turn the fellow's place inside out. And, by God, we will find the evidence we need."

It was stunning, Ghote thought. Once stated, it had all the simpleness and obviousness that marked out the really new discovery. Why, oh why, had he not been able to think of such an idea himself? To have come to the Bats with such a gift offering: it would have established him at once and forever.

And then the dark thought intervened: he had not come to the Bats to bring ideas, however brilliant. He had come to look at such men as Inspector Kelkar with the jaundiced eye of constant and unbiased suspicion.

Yet there would be some use for good ideas. He was to some extent the victim of suspicion himself. DSP Naik certainly believed him to be the beneficiary of some favouritism. He could quiet such suspicions by showing himself to be an active and energetic officer. Now.

He ought at this moment to leap in and add some useful contribution to Kelkar's plan. What? What? Wait, surely he must know someone in his home life who had a relative working in the UK. The people who went there did not all come from the dry and dusty villages of the Punjab. Was there not someone, even living quite close to his own—

"Sir. DSP Naik, sir."

Ghote jerked up at the loud voice. It was Inspector Radwan. He had bounced to his feet even, in his eagerness.

"Sir. DSP. I have no doubt I could lay my hands on half a dozen such fellows right here in Bombay. Near where I live, even. Just once I know where it is I am going to be allocated a quarter."

The DSP smiled in evident pleasure at such keenness.

"As to that, Radwan," he said, "I can give you an answer here and now. The chitty came through just before this meeting."

He pattered about the paper-strewn surface of his big desk and eventually located the memo he wanted.

"Yes," he said. "Government Quarters No 4."

Ghote had somehow known that these were going to be the DSP's words. And he knew too, at once, precisely which house in Government Quarters No 4 was going to go to this boisterous and pushing Muslim. It would be the one that looked across the road exactly on to his own. It would be the house occupied until a few weeks earlier by another Muslim, quiet old Inspector Barmukh, now retired.

"Yes," said the DSP. "It is Number 38-stroke-104."

The very house.

Ghote found himself seized with quite unjustifiable fury. A flurry of blows in the contest he hardly knew he was fighting.

VI

Forceful and direct though Inspector Kelkar's plan to get to the heart of one of the black-money syndicates through foreign exchange was, it took time to bring results. But this was almost inevitable, Ghote reflected as the days went by. Little cotton threads by the dozen were there to be gently tugged. But in the nature of things hardly had they begun to lead in the right direction when time and again they parted.

People who were receiving money from the UK through channels that were unofficial, and indeed illegal, were almost always alert as jungle animals to any hint of danger. When questioned, blank denials soon sprang up. And it was no use persisting then. Threats would have produced more information in ninety-nine cases out of a hundred. But threats are noisy. And if the Kelkar plan was to succeed no one must get to hear that the Black-money and Allied Transactions Squad was interested in this field.

So during the weeks, as September moved into October, it was nothing but frustration for them all. In a Bombay no longer cooled by even the least and last of the monsoon rain, growing hotter and hotter each member of the squad plodded round making careful inquiries in an unobtrusive manner at the homes of people all over the city and often a good way out of it.

Ghote took his full share, as well as making opportunities to linger in the office and pursue his real task. Soon he felt permanently tired. His legs ached even when he got up in the morning and scarcely ceased to ache in the evenings when his wife assiduously pressed and massaged them. A permanent patch of prickly heat seemed to lie across his bony shoulders and no amount of applications of Nycil powder eased it, though the odour of sandalwood that he carried about with him proved a blessing when duty took him to some crazily leaning building in the most crowded part of the city to toil up stairs splashed thickly with red spatters of expectorated betel-chewing with each open doorway tangy with the smell of overcrowded humanity.

But it was something else that took it out of him more than any of this. Once a week it was his duty to report to Mr. Rao.

The meetings took place at a different location each time. And there was always about them an air of hurry, a quick furtiveness that went uncomfortably with Mr. Rao's tall upright figure and long, calm, iron-grey moustachioed face. Ghote knew that precautions were necessary. If someone who was acquainted with them both happened to see them together they would talk. Whole powder trains of suspicion would run to and fro. But the atmosphere of unceasing jumpiness at the meetings made it even more difficult for him to say what he had to. Especially as, fundamentally, as week succeeded week and meeting meeting, he had nothing whatever to say.

"You have noticed nothing, man?" Mr. Rao barked at their fifth encounter, after having said, tersely, that the discreet investigations he was having made into the private circumstances of the other Bats had still produced no fact to stir any legitimate suspicion.

They were in a quiet corner of the Hanging Gardens up on Malabar Hill. It was evening and a great angular frangipani, now in full bloom, was making the fresh darkness densely sweet with the odour from its waxy white trumpets. Its languor contrasted all too sharply with the plain irritation in Mr. Rao's question.

"Sir," Ghote said in answer. "I spend all the time I can watching when plans and results are being discussed. I take every advantage of the office being empty to go through desks. I investigate wastepaper baskets even. But I have also to carry out the tasks allocated to me by DSP Naik, sir."

"The DSP? He's deliberately getting you out of the way?"

The query shot out like a snake's tongue into the blossom-sweet air.

"No, sir. There is definitely no question of that. I had asked myself if it was happening. But when I compared my duties with the others I found that we are working equal hours exactly."

"Very well. But do not leave the possibility out of account. Suspect everybody, Inspector. Suspect everybody."

The words echoed afterwards like a refrain in his head. Conscientiously each time he heard them he made himself hold up to some X-ray camera in his brain one by one each of the Bats. DSP Naik. Inspector Kelkar, ever trim fighting frigate despite the heat and the smells and the dirt. Inspector Nadkarni, never complaining though he had a right to be doing less wearyingly unpleasant work in these last months of his service. Or goose-craning Dayabhai Patel, always it seemed with some new story of the iniquities of the big city. Or Inspector Radwan.

Trying to penetrate the image of Inspector Radwan took it out of him more than considering any of the others. Not because he respected or liked the man. But for the very opposite reason. Daily more and more he was growing to hate him.

The blows now were beginning to tell.

From the moment he had heard that the fellow was to have the house opposite he had known he would be no quiet neighbour. And it had proved absolutely so. Old Inspector Barmukh had produced a gruffly polite greeting for any member of the family he had happened to encounter. But he would have no more thought of presenting himself at the house than he would have set up as an eve-teaser and made himself a nuisance to the passing girls. Radwan—"But, my friend, you must be calling me Rohit"—was different. From the very first day he and his wife had arrived he had been a constant visitor to the house.

There had been good reasons, of course. There were things to ask about the neighbourhood. How near was the nearest doctor? Radwan's wife, it came out, suffered from poor health and their children were with the inspector's mother. What was the best place to buy vegetables? Where did you go for new gas cylinders for the cooking stove?

And there were things to borrow. And to bring back.

Ghote had swung between the immediate conviction that a screwdriver lent would never be seen again to an irritated, but never voiced, desire that the borrowed tool should be kept until there was at least little likelihood of its being almost immediately wanted once more.

"The chap is at the door every ten minutes," he said to his wife. She laughed.

"Oh, it is not so bad as that. And he is pleasant always."

"Yes. He has got plenty to be pleasant about, with each and every one of my tools in his house already."

"But he has just brought back screwdriver. And he was very grateful for the advice I gave about Doctor Das."

"And how long was he here asking? When I am working myself to the bone only, he is here lounging and drinking tea. Why did his wife not come to ask about doctor?"

"The poor woman is not well. That is why Rohit wanted to know about Doctor Das."

"Rohit. Rohit. Did you ever call Inspector Barmukh Salim? What is this Rohit?"

"It is his name. He asked us to call him by it. And that is very friendly."

"It is too friendly."

Indeed, an open breach might have come about except that on the occasions when Ghote ventured to let his feelings appear Rohit Radwan overrode any sharpness in his tone so breezily that there had been little he could do. And then, some six weeks after the Radwans had arrived in the house opposite, two events seemed to take the heat out of the situation.

The first was that Radwan announced that he was sending his wife for a short holiday up into the hills at Mahableshwar. And the second was that at last one of the soft cotton threads at which the Bats had been gently plucking seemed really to be leading somewhere.

It had been Dayabhai Patel, once again, who had set them off on the trail. He had come to Ghote and confided that he thought he was on to a good prospect. He wanted Ghote's opinion on the spot. And Ghote knew why. A week before Dayabhai had announced at one of DSP Naik's conferences that he had a lead. With excitement sending the blood up into his round face the DSP had ordered all the rest of the Bats to stand by. And it had turned out that Dayabhai had got hold of a prostitute in a house off Grant Road and that she had by way of a joke led him on and on with skilfully unspecific promises to provide the information he seemed to be seeking. It had taken Inspector Nadkarni more than an hour of patient questioning to get the truth from the creature. So Dayabhai had good reason to be cautious.

His new find lived in one of those niches of almost primitive life that nestle in the heart of brash, clacking, cosmopolitan Bombay. She was the wife of one of a community of fisherfolk tucked away on the seaward slope of Malabar Hill beneath the big blocks of softly coloured new apartments and the great, old, wooden-balconied houses of the maharajahs and the big film stars. Her son, Dayabhai had learnt—or, Ghote wondered had he been fed the tale?—had shown unusual enterprise and got himself to England. He was working in a factory there now and sending what seemed like huge sums back to his family leading the hazardous life shared by frail-boated fishermen everywhere. Dayabhai's careful preliminary talk with the mother had seemed to show her as altogether too ignorant not to confide in a friendly inquirer apparently seeking the same benefits.

Ghote smiled to himself a little grimly as he walked with Dayabhai at the agreed time that evening down the only road leading to this village-within-a-city, a sloping lane intersected with occasional rough steps. Their informant sounded innocent enough: but was the man who had got the information from her much less simple and trusting despite the progress he seemed to have made since their college days?

They came to the village, hardly lit at all but clearly to be seen in the strong pearly moonlight. It was set round a very old, unexpectedly large tank, the steps leading down into its water broken and uneven. On the far side was a temple, as old as the tank, and in a poor state of repair. But it was still clearly much used. There was a statue on the far wall, visible through the main arch, and in front of it were offerings, small indeterminate piles and withered garlands. As they walked nearer, it was possible to make out by the glow of a charcoal brazier beside the statue that fresh red kumkum had been smeared on it. It represented a woman, full-breasted and slim-waisted. She seemed to Ghote to convey great serenity and a confidence beyond the storms of the day. Could he really see in the charcoal glow her faint and ever-welcoming smile?

To either side of the tank there were the huts of the villagers, leaf-roofed shacks with no windows and low open doorways. Above them grew a few ragged palms. Between the mouth of the lane they had come down and the low broken parapet of the tank was the village bazaar, a pathetic collection of eight or nine stalls one of which was no more than a piece of gunny stretched on the ground with on it a few heaps of half-rotten or wholly withered vegetables.

There were quite a number of people about, as well as naked children running to and fro. In the precious hours of daylight anyone as poor as the villagers had no time for the sociability of buying and selling.

"It is the paan stall there to the right," Dayabhai said quietly.

"All right," Ghote answered. "Come on."

"No, a word first."

Dayabhai put a restraining hand on his arm.

"Listen, old chap," he said quietly. "A word of warning."

Is he going to tell me how to conduct an interview with a frightened witness, Ghote thought. He felt a sense of slight outrage.

"Well?" he said.

"It is this, old boy. Do not, whatever you do, buy any paans from her. Yesterday I took three or four. I thought it would assist me to gain her confidence. But they must have been appallingly dirty. I have been suffering the most acute internal botheration all today."

Ghote smiled to himself in the darkness.

"Thank you for the tip," he said.

"Not at all, bhai. Come on then."

Dayabhai squared his shoulders, sending his wrists protruding even further from his shirtsleeves. Then he advanced towards the bazaar like a ramparts-scaling soldier worsted once but not to be beaten.

The enemy, when they came to her stall, proved to be a creature of the utmost timidity. Stinking of fish.

Both qualities, Ghote reflected, were to be expected. Everyone in the village, no doubt, would stink of the fish that was their livelihood. And, for this woman, living perhaps all her time in the enclosed little community, it was reasonable enough to be permeated with suspicions for anybody coming from outside.

Her shyness did, however, make things difficult. The day before Dayabhai had succeeded in ingratiating himself far enough with her to learn most but not all of the details about how she got the money that came from her adventurous son in England. No doubt his boyish innocence had paid off with that, Ghote thought. If ever there was anyone who looked as if he needed a mother to keep him out of unfortunate experiences, it was Dayabhai.

But tonight his own arrival, in the guise of Dayabhai's elder brother, there to learn of the wonder for himself, had set back relations right to the beginning.

So with the utmost patience—constantly bringing to mind old Nadkarni and his way of going about things—Ghote set out to establish warmth of feeling between himself and the gaunt but deer-shrinking keeper of the paan stall. He did not go so far as to buy one of the three paans set out under the dully burning light of a kerosene lamp on the crude bench that constituted her stall. But he did purchase a single betel leaf to chew. And later he ventured on a leaf-wrapped bidi to smoke, though it was all he could do to puff its acrid fumes with an appearance of pleasure.

He made himself do it, however. He was lulling bit by bit those suspicions of anything from outside that lay all-too-easy-to-wake so near the surface of his witness' mind. And he was not going to spoil the work.

For more than an hour they talked about the pleasures of chewing betel and of smoking, the price of fish and the dangers of a fisherman's life, the monsoon that had just finished and the effects good and bad that it had had. Then at last Ghote felt able to work round to talk of the cost-of-living in general.

And twenty minutes later he was hearing full details in the strongly accented Marathi it had taken him long enough to get used to about the man who brought money "from my boy across the black water." It had been at once apparent that this time Dayabhai had struck authentic gold.

Here was an informant simply too innocent not to trust them, once they had gone to enough trouble to earn that trust. Here was the beginning of a trail that ought to lead from this fish-stinking village right up to the seth cynically engaged in making himself yet richer by transforming legally gained sums made in distant England into the secret, illegal, hidden power of black money.

"And, Ama," Ghote was able to ask finally, "when does this man come to you with the money?"

"It is once every month."

"Yes. But when in the month, Ama?"

"It is the same time always."

"Ah, yes. Yes. But on which day?"

"Oh, days I am not knowing."

"Then how do you—"

Ghote stopped himself. He must not drop back into the methods of the interrogation room. This was not the time to seize on any apparent weakness in logic and pursue it till the whole lie was brought to light. In all probability this timid gaunt creature on the bench beside him did not know the days of the month at all.

"Yes," he said gently. "And is it long since he came last?"

"Oh, it is long. Already it is very long. He will come tomorrow. Or the day after. Tomorrow he will come."

"And when in the day does he come, Ama?"

"At the end of it always."

It proved to be not the next day but the day following that the regular visitor to the fishing village made his call. But when he did so he came in exactly the fashion Dayabhai Patel's informant had said that he would. And the Bats were hidden there to see him come and to follow him as he left.

The operation was commanded by Inspector Kelkar, that smooth grained rock of reliability. It was a model of how such a thing should be done.

In the period before the earlier of the two times they had been given for the black-money sub-agent to pay his visit the whole village was discreetly surveyed. Every possible approach to it was checked. Finally comprehensive plans were made for a watch from midafternoon onwards.

Nor did Inspector Kelkar neglect security. There was not one single written word about any aspect of the operation. And, when they were discussing plans behind the locked door of the Bats office, Kelkar even carried out a preliminary check against possible bugging. Each of them, however unnecessarily, had been personally warned by DSP Naik against saying anything at all about the affair to anybody.

"You are not even to warn your wives that you will be late back home," he said. His round face was solemn as a clock.

Ghote heard him with a matching solemnity. And he recorded that, if some breach of security allowed their man to escape again this time, it would be beyond doubt one of their number, one of the five of them, who would be responsible. It might be poor Dayabhai, even though he had found this so promising trail for them. Or it might be Radwan, contemptuously confident though he was that they were at last about to pull off a major success. Or it might be old Nadkarni, and it would prove true that at the end of his service he had been cunningly piling up a small fortune to make his retirement days easy. Or it might be Kelkar himself, and all the effort and dash he was putting into the operation would turn out to have been only a supremely efficient bluff. Or could it be the DSP even, his solemn warnings mere hypocrisy?

And, no doubt, the others were even at this moment probing at him himself with a thousand darts of wild suspicion.

Nothing, however, seemed to go wrong with the operation in any way. The sub-agent bringing the black money to the village was easily spotted as he approached. He was quietly followed when he left. He was tracked without difficulty to a room in a tall, crazily leaning house filled all day with the continuous *plonk-plonk* of coppersmiths' hammers from the Bendhi Bazaar. And from there he was followed later to a house in the once fashionable and still prosperous suburb of Matunga, a house which he could have no likely reason for visiting.

This proved to belong to an individual whom the neighbours could describe no more accurately than as "businessman." But whatever business it was he transacted it apparently brought him in plenty. He had a car, "foreign also." But evidently he hardly depended on it for his livelihood since he made only rare excursions. Yet his wife had so many gold bangles she could hardly lift her arms, the envious neighbours said. And his children went to an expensive missionary school.

More important to the Bats, however, was the information that, besides the man they had tracked to the house, a number of others also called there regularly and left again soon afterwards.

"It all adds up," Inspector Kelkar said, the light of the chase plainer and plainer to see on his crisply sideboarded face.

"This foreign car?" the DSP asked. "Can we find out exactly what make it is?"

Inspector Kelkar answered without a trace of a proud smile.

"It is an Opel Rekord, about seven or eight years old. Red. The number is MRP 12 something. The boy I talked with was not sure of the last figure."

"Never mind," said the DSP. "We would be able to spot that with no trouble whatsoever. And I like the sound of those occasional outings the fellow takes. I like them very much indeed."

So, each member of the Bats equipped with his own vehicle, they waited at chosen points near the house in Matunga. And on the third day the man whom they now felt certain was one of the important agents of a big black-money syndicate happily drove past the place where Inspector Kelkar himself was waiting. And he was driving the unmistakable red Opel Rekord.

Ghote, allocated now an Ambassador in very reasonable condition in place of his ill-fated Standard, following in his turn at a discreet distance, could not resist, in this privacy, letting a smile come to his lips. A tigerish smile even.

Once again, guilelessly, he turned to fight what he still thought of as the real enemy. And once more the adversary who had already landed more than one body blow, for all that Ghote had hardly noticed, gained from his innocence new reserves of punishing strength.

But Ghote had thoughts only for the present.

The Bats had found their tiny thread of visible cotton. They had teased at it and gently tugged at it. And it had held until it had led them to the next stage. There they had surrounded the syndicate's sub-agent with a web of watchfulness that had taken them to Matunga and the next man in the chain. And now . . . Now, surely, this agent was leading them to the next final stage.

The head of the syndicate himself, the seth, would soon be within their grasp. Time to throw away mutual distrust now. Time for action, pure action.

VII

The action that came when the Bats' nets were hemming in the seth from every side was, as it turned out, about as far removed as possible from what Ghote had envisaged. He found himself taking part in a duel. A duel with a woman. With a siren of a woman.

Their trailing of the agent from the big house in Matunga had led them to Malabar Hill, perched coolly above the teeming city, the vast stretch of the Arabian Sea on one side and the placid waters of Back Bay on the other. The Opel Rekord had come to a halt outside a rosy pink block of towering flats. Inspector Kelkar had had a short and forceful conversation with the gorgeously uniformed and turbaned chaprassi who presided over the block's entrance hall. He had emerged with two decidedly interesting facts. The first was that this was not the only time the agent in the Opel had visited the flats and that it was to the topmost one of all, the luxury penthouse, that he went. The second fact was that the owner of this penthouse, a certain Mr. Baddu Pujari, kept there a mistress.

"A mistress," Inspector Kelkar had said sternly as they gathered round him in the concealment of a group of abundant flowering bushes in front of the neighbouring flats block. "If we needed further confirmation that this Pujari fellow is our man, that is it."

DSP Naik almost hopped up and down with pleasure.

"Did you find out anything more about Pujari himself?" he asked.

"Only that he is fat," Kelkar, that spruce person, replied. "According to the chaprassi he is so fat he cannot get into a car even."

"Look. Look."

It was Sub-Inspector Patel, who had been detailed by the DSP to keep an eye on the Opel while the rest of them were giving Kelkar their full attention.

They all swung round.

"I do not think it is right what you have been saying, Inspector Kelkar," Dayabhai said.

He was pointing over at the roadway outside the rosy-pink block, and they saw that his high-handedness towards the magnificent Kelkar was justified. The owner of the Opel Rekord, still clutching the brief case which he had taken with him up to the flat though it was now presumably empty, was solicitously holding wide the car's nearside front door. And a man of truly immense bulk was succeeding, bit by bit, in squeezing himself into the vehicle.

The very difficulty he was having proved him to be, nevertheless, the Baddu Pujari whom the chaprassi had declared could never get inside a car. He was an extraordinary shape. Though for mere fatness, mere belly-projection, he was not perhaps grosser than some other overfed Bombay businessman, for breadth of body from arm to arm he must surely be unbeatable. His back, twisted and turned in his efforts to slide himself into the heavily canting Opel, was one solid rounded wall of stretched cloth. Ghote calculated that his jacket, by its glint made of pure silk, would if supported by a convenient length of stout bamboo form a tent that could easily take his own son stretched out at full length to sleep under its shade.

At last the immense creature finally proved by this exceptional performance the chaprassi's rule about his bulk. With a last great sucking heave he slid his second vast ham on to the Opel's seat and then drew in after it a pillar-thick leg. The car's owner closed its door on him with infinite precaution. He hurried round to the driving side.

"Yes," said Inspector Nadkarni, with a little dry cough, "but when it comes to it are we going to find that the engine is jammed against the roadway beneath?"

They waited in silence to discover. The supposition did not seem in any way too fantastic.

But the Opel did start. And it was able to move off, though it was plainly tipped towards the near side.

"Now," snapped Inspector Kelkar. "This is our chance."

"Our chance, Kelkar?" the DSP asked.

"To get at the mistress," Kelkar said. "Sir, that woman will know where he keeps his hoard of black money. And it is almost bound to be in the flat. The fellow has to keep it somewhere."

It was true, Ghote reflected. No black-money seth could just take his wealth to a bank. He had to keep somewhere or other the actual wads of notes, green dollars, blue British five-pound notes or big high-denomination rupee notes. It was the one clear advantage the forces of order had in their battle with this subversion.

"Then we must get a search warrant," the DSP said firmly.

"Yes, yes, of course, DSP," Kelkar answered. "But that will take time. I suggest Sub-Inspector Patel drives you down at once to apply. But in the meanwhile one of us must interview the mistress. She will know where he has his hiding place. If Pujari comes back before we find out, he is going to have so many lawyers in the place we shall never get him even with a warrant."

"Kelkar, you are right. Patel, come with me. Kelkar, I leave to you the choice of whoever is to deal with the lady."

And, the moment the DSP had bustled off, Ghote volunteered. He did not need to say he saw this as his chance to redeem his failure at a woman's hands in their last attempt to rout out a seth. It was plain from the quick assessing glance that Kelkar gave him that this was being taken into account.

"Right then, Ghote. I think you will have the spirit for this."

There were only a few moments for preparation. Kelkar suggested he had better pose as a Customs investigator—"Show her your own warrant card if she asks: a woman like that would not know the difference"—and claim it had come to Customs' notice that she was in possession of smuggled items. It was, Kelkar added, almost certain to be in fact the case.

Less than two minutes later a smartly uniformed, padding, barefoot servant was showing him into the drawing room of the flat, all ornate decoration and heavily framed mirrors. And Baddu Pujari's mistress was stretched in front of him, reclining at full length on a divan, a sprawl of soft cushions at her head.

She was, disturbingly, both younger and older than he had been expecting. Younger, in that somehow he had thought she was going to be a creature of infinite resource, a temptress practised through the years in the arts of her profession. Older, in that when he had thought of the enormous Baddu Pujari he could not imagine any woman of his other than as a toy, or even a sweetmeat, something tender and to be gobbled.

But Meena—Meena Miss, the servant had called her—was certainly not to be gobbled. There was a litheness about her that put any such thoughts completely out of the mind. Yet the litheness was also the litheness of youth. She must, Ghote reckoned in a sudden sweat of crude arithmetic, be somewhere about twenty-five. And she had tremendous sex appeal.

It exuded from her. It poured silkily off every inch of the hip-hugging, bright shocking-pink trousers she wore—bell-bottoms, Ghote registered, they are called bell-bottoms—and it wafted, different but equally effective, from the frothy, lacy pink blouse that drew attention to a richly swelling bosom much more than it discreetly covered it. The profusion of heavy jewellery on her fingers, at her ears and round her neck clinked and sparkled sex appeal. A brutally direct and musky scent signalled the same blatant message.

"Good day, madam," Ghote said.

Meena surveyed him. She said nothing.

Moment by moment he became more and more conscious of every deficiency in his appearance. His trousers, although they were one of his new pairs—he had not worn the old ones once since he had begun his double duties with the Bats—were very crushed in the front. From the clammy coldness at his armpits he knew that there were two large sweat patches on his shirt. His shoulders were too thin. His face lacked any real signs of aggressive masculinity.

"Sulu said it was Customs matter," Meena pronounced at last, pouting her full lips.

Well, he thought, at least she appears not to have any suspicion of the real purpose of my visit. She cannot be too much in Pujari's confidence then, or an unknown inquirer coming poking in like this would have her running to telephone a lawyer.

He decided to work on the assumption that she was essentially innocent.

"Well, yes, madam," he said, "it is a question of smuggled goods. It is particularly a matter of watches that we are inquiring into. May I ask is that watch you are wearing foreign?"

Meena extended a long bare arm ringed at the soft biceps by a gold slave bangle and with a tiny watch almost lost in a heavy gold band at the wrist.

"But, of course, it is foreign," she said. "I am crazy, crazy for foreign."

"May I conduct examination?" Ghote asked.

Immediately he regretted this touch of realism. And, an instant before he had actually produced it, it had seemed so cunningly formed to allay every lingering suspicion.

Meena smiled at him. He had known that she would.

"But, yes, look, look, Mr. Customs Man," she said. "But come here and look."

The fine wrist twisted this way and that. Ghote marched up to the divan with its array of sprawling silk cushions. He bent stiffly from the waist and gave the watch on that gently oscillating wrist a perfunctory glare.

"Yes," he grated out. "The article would appear to be of foreign manufacture. May I ask where it was that you obtained?"

Meena gave a low throaty chuckle.

"But of course," she answered, "it was my little Baddu that gave."

"Your little Baddu?"

Ghote was for a moment genuinely mystified. His mind could not make any connection between the wall-gigantic Baddu Pujari and the figure conjured up by Meena's words.

"He is very kind," Meena added.

And at this the whole life lived in this heavily decorated, softly luxurious place sprang into Ghote's mind. Hotly he drove himself away from any contemplation of the final point of it all.

He forced himself to put another question, though his voice came out absurdly high and choked.

"Your little Baddu is Mr. Baddu Pujari, owner of this flat?"

"Yes, yes, of course."

"And can you inform where the said Mr. Pujari purchased the article?"

But he had not been thinking enough. Even Meena's sense of self-preservation was aroused at this.

"Where he is purchasing?" she shot back. "But you must not try to find that out, Mr. Customs Man."

"But why not?" Ghote asked.

Meena smiled at him. He realised how very long her eyelashes were. Such things were manufactured surely?

"But never must a girl ask such things of her man," Meena breathed. "Am I asking such things of you?"

"But— But I have given nothing," Ghote said, feeling himself slide away on a sea of illogicalities.

"No," Meena said softly.

She dropped her head back on the heap of soft cushions. Her full bosom rose with the sureness of twin suns thrusting upwards over the horizon.

"No," she said. "You have not given. But if you had . . . And you would like, isn't it? You would like to give some nice gift to Meena?"

An attempt was being made at seduction, Ghote registered. This woman—there could be no doubt about it—was blatantly attempting to seduce him. It was outrageous. When he told Protima she would be furious.

Perhaps he had better not tell Protima.

The quick jab left its bruise low on the ribs.

"There is no question of the giving of gifts," he said, standing almost to attention in an effort to achieve the utmost correctness of manner. "May I remind, I am a poli— I am a Customs officer making inquiries."

"But at least you could be comfortable to make," Meena said, standing.

Her voice was crooning. Crooning. It was disgraceful. And it was of no use for her to move over like that to make a space on the divan. Of no use whatsoever.

He stood still and thundered out a demand.

"I have asked where Mr. Pujari obtained that watch."

"Oh, Mr. Customs Man. Mr. Customs Man, you are so cruel. You are making poor Meena so unhappy."

Ghote drew in a long breath and gathered new strength.

"I would not make unhappy if you would provide answer to my question," he said.

"But how can I do that?"

Meena had swirled in one supple movement into a sitting position. All the languor had left her wide, kohl-darkened eyes.

"How can I? How can I? How am I knowing what he is doing all the time? I am telling you sometimes he goes out on business —business. Like now. He is out now, isn't it?"

"He appears to be absent, certainly," Ghote said, delighted at his own adroitness in conveying that his call had been made at this time purely by chance.

"Yes, he is out now. But even when he is here, how can I all the time be knowing what he is doing?"

The drifting stream of her mind had produced this heaven-sent chance. Ghote grabbed at it.

"Knowing what he is doing?" he said. "On the contrary, madam, it would seem to me that there would not be many occasions when you were absent from the gentleman in question."

He felt the crude brutality of what he had just said ringing round the ornate, mirror-thick, plumply carpeted room. Ought he to have assumed so much knowledge of her private life? What would her reaction be if she and Mr. Pujari were good friends only?

"But, no, Mr. Customs Man. No, that is not so."

Yet she showed no trace of anger. In fact, she was back to crooning.

"No, that is where you are wrong, Mr. Customs Man. Often and often is my little Baddu hiding from me here."

"Hiding from you?" Ghote said incredulously. "But where? Where could he hide?"

He looked round the heavily luxurious room. A vision of the gigantic Mr. Pujari endeavouring to crouch behind one of the much-tasselled, velvet-covered armchairs came into his mind. A baby elephant would have had as much difficulty.

"But in the bathroom always he is hiding," Meena said. "For so long he is in there. And it is not when he is having bath. We take bath always together."

She looked at Ghote with a smile of such coyness that he could have hit her. But abruptly it was replaced by a look of pure crosspatch perplexity.

"But what does he do in there?" she said. "He is in it so long, and he will not speak to his Meena even. Mr. Customs Man, I am wondering and wondering what it is he is doing. Can you tell me what? Please, mister, can you suggest anything?"

Ghote could easily have suggested what Mr. Pujari might be doing locked in his bathroom away from Meena's prying eyes. But it was the last thing he wanted her to guess.

He rapidly puffed up his chest and shouted at her instead a further demand to be told where Mr. Pujari had obtained her foreign watch. It was not very subtle. But it was the best he could do. And all he could think of after that was to repeat the question several times more in different forms.

But in the course of all his hectoring he actually received a bonus to the revelation Meena had already given him: the disclosure that, although her "little Baddu" was prodigal with gifts of all sorts she never once had had from him any cash.

At last he felt that he had said enough to disguise from his witness the importance of what she had told him. He contrived some parting threat and left.

His report to Inspector Kelkar in the shadow of the bushes in front of the next-door block was simple and brief.

"Inspector, the cash is in the bathroom. I am sure of it. But it will be well hidden there."

He had hardly finished when, with a squealing of brakes, Dayabhai Patel's car drew up, though with DSP Naik alone in it. He bounded out and came over to them, actually waving the search warrant.

"We go in straightaway, DSP?" Kelkar asked.

"Yes, yes, Inspector."

"And Patel, where is he?"

The DSP gave a short laugh, with a hint of disapproval in it.

"That stomach of his," he said. "I suspect he is not a fellow who keeps himself in tiptop form."

Poor Dayabhai, Ghote thought. Unlucky indeed to have fallen foul already of the DSP's well-known mania for keep-fit. Especially when his stomach trouble had actually been acquired on active service among the dirt-rich paans of the woman who had put them at last on this trail.

But there was no time to waste on sympathy with Dayabhai now. Briefly Inspector Kelkar told the DSP what they thought the hiding place of the black money in Baddu Pujari's flat would prove to be. Then the whole body of them moved off determinedly towards the rosy-pink block and the penthouse at the top of it.

VIII

They burst in all in a bunch, pushing the servant out of the way and going at once to flourish the search warrant under the nose of Meena. She had actually risen from her divan at the sound of their entry and the servant's frightened squawk. She stood and stared at them now, without a word to say. Even the fact that among these CID officers was the Customs man who had a few minutes earlier survived her wiles did not bring from her any protest.

But they had no time to bother with her. Inspector Nadkarni stayed with her to make sure she did not use the telephone and the rest of them piled into the bathroom.

It was, to Ghote's somewhat jaundiced eyes, an altogether excessively large and fantastically luxurious place. There was a sunken central tub, more than big enough for the baths for two that Meena had so coyly referred to. The walls, which were tiled from floor to ceiling, had pictures of swaying nautch girls on them. There was a deeply recessed shower cubicle with an underwater sea scene on its tiles. Both this and the bath had fittings glitteringly plated in gold. There was a whole zoo full of lions' heads on the wall, each grasping a gold ring from which cascaded a towel of immense size and fluffiness. There was a bar. There was a medicine cupboard that was almost as big and as well stocked. There were no fewer than three cork-topped stools as well as a massive cork-seated armchair. There was a metal stand that held sponges of half a dozen different shapes and colours, all enormous, and an array of brushes for scrubbing the nails, scrubbing the back, scrubbing the soles of the feet.

Inspector Kelkar gave it all one sweeping glance.

"Right," he said.

And swiftly and economically he detailed separate tasks for each of them.

"Move everything that can be moved," he concluded. "If it will unscrew, unscrew it. Press every panel. Twist every knob."

They set to work. The lushly gold-plated fittings were tugged this way and that until they proved immovable or came off in the process. The whole glass-topped bar was taken to pieces by Inspector Radwan and every bottle in it was shaken till it frothed in case it hid a key. Ghote himself gave the same treatment to the many medicines in their large cupboard, though without feeling it necessary to comment on the contents. He even succeeded in heaving the whole cupboard clear of the wall. Every sponge in the metal stand was personally squeezed by the DSP.

But nothing came to light.

Inspector Kelkar was, however, undismayed.

"All right," he said. "But that black money was not going to be just where we would find it for the asking. We are not playing with a child only. So now we are really going to take this place to pieces. Ghote, go out and see if you can find some tools. Or knives from the kitchen. Every one of these tiles is coming off for a start."

Ghote managed to get hold of a fine assortment of screwdrivers and heavy kitchen knives and they all set to work hard as they could go. Soon the once luxurious bathroom resembled nothing so much as a building site. The whole sunken double bath was filled with objects wrenched from their setting. There were heaps of tiles in crazily tilting piles all over the floor. Pipes and tangled electric cables leaned out of the walls. There was a thick haze of white dust everywhere.

It was Kelkar himself, when they were about halfway through, who made the discovery.

"Aha."

His cry rang out above the noise of scraping and scratching tools, of grunting and labouring hackers. They all turned towards him.

He was standing on one of the cork-topped stools, holding in both hands the head of the shower which he had torn by main force from its fitting flush with the ceiling of the shower recess. A deep black hole could be seen above him.

"Noticed when I got to this," he said, giving the shower head a shake, "that there were no marks of water on its surface. Guessed there would be something behind it."

He held out the shower head for someone to take from him. Ghote stepped forward and put it on the glass top of the dismantled bar which had been balanced on the arms of the cork-seated chair.

Inspector Kelkar flexed his knees and thrust his head up into the dark recess.

"Hm?"

His voice boomed from inside the hole. Boomed with an unexpected note of inquiry.

There was a moment of silence. Then Kelkar spoke again.

"Someone come and collect these," he said.

Again Ghote stepped forward. Into his outstretched hands Kelkar put three solidly bound, gold-edged books and one small elaborately shaped bottle.

"That is all," his muffled voice came from the hole.

Ghote set out the haul on the bar-top beside the shower head. He opened one of the books. They saw a pornographic drawing of crystal-clear explicitness. Ghote picked up the bottle and looked at its label. It was richly printed. It said that the contents were: "The Sovereign Rejuvenatory Fluid—All that is rare in the Aphrodisiac Science—Pure gold, the ground whiskers of the Royal Tiger, Asses' Milk, the powdered horn of the Great African Rhinoceros."

"There was nothing more hidden up there?" he asked in dismay, at once regretting the lack of trust this showed in Inspector Kelkar.

But Kelkar, considerably dismayed himself, did not take offence.

"No, nothing more," he said.

He looked round at them all.

"Well," he added, "I suppose we had better finish the job. It is possible he hides black money here as well. Though . . ."

Quite uncharacteristically his voice tailed off. But he had only expressed what they were all feeling. And nor did the completion of their demolition task on the bathroom prove them wrong. There was nothing else hidden there.

But the acknowledgement of that was not their worst moment. That came two minutes later. There was the sound of a sharp voice in the hallway of the flat and then the bathroom door was flung open to reveal the enormous bulk of a totally outraged Baddu Pujari.

The post-mortem on the disaster had been an even more depressed occasion than that after the smugglers' car fiasco six weeks before. And with good reason. Baddu Pujari had proved to be one of those people with a talent for making a fuss. And he had made a colossal fuss over what Inspector Kelkar had done to his bathroom. Even before they could get away from the penthouse it had taken all DSP Naik's mournful dignity and all Inspector Nadkarni's patient thrusting forward of their search warrant. And, as the DSP had said, he would be spending all his time for days to come in top-level conference to make sure the matter was eventually dealt with quietly. Let alone the heavy drain on the Secret Sources fund that would be required.

But even more depressing than the failure itself was the implication behind it. Once more, almost for certain, the Bats had been betrayed.

There was the possibility still, as DSP Naik had taken care to point out, that Baddu Pujari was a perfectly honest businessman, even if his sexual morals were not perfect. It was possible that the affair had gone wrong only because Inspector Kelkar had been too vigorous in pursuing it. Ghote sadly acknowledged to himself the force of this. It was magnificent to be as thrusting as Kelkar was, but there was always the chance that he would thrust too soon and too hard and land up in trouble.

And then the niggling thought followed that perhaps a man of Kelkar's tremendous drive was not really right for the police. It was necessary as a policeman to keep within certain bounds. And if Kelkar had long been frustrated by such restriction . . . Was it possible that the very virtues of the man had swept him onwards beyond the bounds of order?

At that moment Ghote had felt a scalding fury with his lot, that it should have driven him feeling to thoughts like that.

But it had. It had taken him to distrust even a man like Inspector Kelkar. It had taken him scampering over every tiny circumstance of the operation that had begun in the fish-smelling atmosphere of the village in an effort to find one give-away error that would point the finger at any one of the Bats. Had there been a period when one of them had been absent from the rest? A time when a telephone call might have been made to some contact in the criminal world?

There had. There had been several short periods even since the time they had firmly come to the conclusion that the house in Matunga was a link in the chain leading to a seth, when each of them had, for what had seemed good and sufficient reasons, been away from the others.

Dayabhai. What about his sudden onset of stomach trouble? That had been the cause of the most notable absence. Had it been put on to give him the opportunity to get in touch with Baddu Pujari himself? And had Pujari then gone hurrying back to the penthouse, created his fuss about his bathroom and saved his black money hidden somewhere else? It was possible. But then it was possible too that he had actually taken the black money away under their very noses in his agent's brief case in the red Opel.

For each of the others there was some similar, if less obvious chance of sending a warning.

Wearily Ghote had set off for home, unable to stop his mind going on and on whirling with suspicions as ominous, as manifold, as overshadowingly dark as the bats that, at that evening hour, were descending all over the city to feed on whatever softly ripe fruit they could smell out.

At home he found, bewilderingly, that the bats that had seemed to throng his mind, appeared to have come to life. The air over the modest roof of his boxy Government Quarters house was thick with them, zooming, dipping, and circling.

He stood and looked at them, puzzled and unhappy. And then he thought of his cherished plantain tree at the back. The creatures would have dug their fangs into every sparse, just-ready, red fruit it bore. He raced into the house. Without stopping to greet either wife or son, he ran on through to the back. And, yes, at least half of the little, hardish, finger-like fruits the tree had painfully produced had been savaged.

"What is it you are looking?"

Protima had followed him out, from the kitchen, wiping her hands on the corner of her sari.

"All these bats," he said. "They have destroyed the plantains. And they were the best crop the tree has ever had."

"But not to worry," Protima answered. "No one ever eats those things."

He whirled round from his careful inspection of the dusty-leaved tree.

"Now you are passing the limit," he snapped. "I eat them always. And Ved is fond of them also."

"Once he ate, yes," Protima said. "But now he never takes. And I am glad. I do not want always to be visiting Doctor Das because he has stomach pain."

"Very well, if Ved does not any longer know what is good, I do. I was looking forward to that fruit. Why have the bats all come here tonight? Have you persuaded to fly this way?"

Protima laughed. With, Ghote thought, more venom than was altogether fitting.

"Why should I persuade?" she said. "If you want to eat those hard little things, eat, eat. I do not care. The way you look after that old tree as if it was a child only. You would never see a man like Rohit do that."

"Rohit? Rohit?" Ghote retorted, feeling a sharp sense of injustice at her using a man like Inspector Radwan to attack him. "What is it Rohit? Why are you mentioning Rohit?"

Protima gave him a glance of victorious scorn.

"Because it is Rohit who is the cause of the bats eating your old tree," she said. "This morning he climbed up and chased them all out of the palms behind his house."

Ghote experienced a deep outrage. He wanted blindly to fight. Not Radwan. Not Protima. But some unknown, dimly guessed-at antagonist.

"But why did Radwan do that?" he spluttered. "There had been bats in those trees for years. Inspector Barmukh was very pleased to have them. Bats are sacred to a Muslim."

Wave on wave of indignation against Rohit Radwan crashed through him. He was just the sort of fellow not to have beliefs. He was probably an atheist. He was irresponsible. It was just like him to take the law into his own hands and disturb bats that had hardly taken other people's fruit for years. He was probably the one who was selling information to the black-money syndicates.

But, at this thought, passion abruptly cooled. The betrayal was altogether a different matter from being a mere public nuisance. That was something deadly serious.

He listened without much attention as Protima went on praising the Muslim as a man of action in contrast with an unnamed person who constantly neglected his wife. Then, without a further word, he went back inside to take a much needed bath and wash away the sweat and stickiness of a long and, in the end, useless day.

But Protima's praise for Radwan nevertheless lodged in his mind. He felt as if he was always swapping blows with some huge and looming opponent, and getting the worst of it. And the more he thought about it all in the days and weeks to come the less he liked it.

It was brought to mind almost every evening indeed by the bats which, routed out by Radwan, established their colony almost directly behind his own house high up under the eaves of a big neglected stone godown that had stood there for a hundred years or more. There they clustered in their dozens protected by the thickly growing leaves of the neem tree just beyond the official limits of Ghote's small compound. He spent some time shortly after their arrival inspecting the heavy masses of monstrous evil-faced creatures as they clung to projections along the top of the godown and among the higher branches of the neem. They had heads, he discovered, like miniature dogs. Or, no, like little jackals. And as the sunlight penetrated to their concealed lair their fur could be seen, as they crawled upside down from place to place shoving and pushing at each other, to be of a reddish hue, a fiercely predatory and fox-like colour.

They stank too. Even through the fresh odour of the neem leaves that had delighted him since he had first come to the house the sharply offensive odour could be detected. But their noise was worse. As soon as dusk grew near it began. An unholy squeaking. The hundred, tiny, individual, sharp bleats combined to form one almost rhythmical, inescapable, monster squeak, repeated and repeated. Never an evening passed without it dinning out at them.

And both Protima and Ved were soon scared stiff of the creatures. Protima swore that one night one of them would get entangled in her hair. The thought of those leathery wings—some of the creatures were a full yard from wingtip to wingtip—beating around one's head while the little claws were caught inescapably in one's hair was, Ghote admitted, enough to produce very real fear in anybody. Ved dreamt of the beasts, and woke up shouting that they were biting him.

Yet often though he contemplated the problem of getting rid of the creatures in the short times he was free both of his official duties and of the secret task that had been imposed on him, he could see no solution. The old stone wall of the godown was blank and smooth and very high. The neem, though it would not be difficult to thrust one's way up into its glossy heart, was at its outer edges far too thin-branched to support even a small boy.

There seemed to be no answer: a fact that did not stop Protima frequently referring to the way Rohit Radwan had dealt with the bats when they were near his house.

Indeed, relations between himself and Protima seemed to have dropped quite suddenly into a long slow slide of broken and uneven going. Sometimes he blamed his long hours of double duty for it. And at other times he wondered whether it was, in fact, those long hours and his drained energies that stopped things getting into a worse state. If he had had time and spirit to fight back, would he not have thrown Rohit Radwan's name back at her? And with what results?

He did not dare to contemplate them. Now, fighting hard daily, he felt the need to back away fists held defensively high.

Certainly, in the months at the beginning of the cool time of year, the months running from October to January, Protima seemed to taunt him more and more frequently with the example of Rohit Radwan. And all he felt able to do in return was to stop himself ever thinking how much of it all was only taunting. He came to welcome any new demands on his time that the Bats made as they succeeded in securing a few minor triumphs.

But these were small affairs indeed, as they all well knew. They were successes that the regular CID or the Customs might have had, things like the discovery in a more or less inept hiding place of a store of black money running to something under a lakh of rupees. There was never anything that got near justifying the setting up of the Bats and the large resources given to them.

And if the Bats had had some successes, however small, he himself in his real task had none at all. Though never a day passed without him doing something to try to sniff out which of his colleagues had betrayed them, he never got the slightest hint of a scent.

Mr. Rao cut down their meetings from once a week to once a fortnight. Then he made them once every three weeks. But whenever and wherever they met, watching the children on the swaying back of the riding elephant in the Victoria Gardens, or mingling with the Bombay City Cup racegoers at Mahalaxmi, or lost in the dense evening crowd amid the flaring naphtha lights of the vendors' stalls on the wide stretch of Apollo Bunder, Ghote had nothing to tell him.

But it was Apollo Bunder one evening, under the towering, golden-stone mass of the Gateway of India with the still waters of the Harbour, black and light-pinpointed behind, that the Bats themselves at last got the hint of a trail that looked as if it might lead them to one of the really big black-money seths.

IX

The spark of new hope that had come to the Bats at last was the result of weeks of work. Inspector Nadkarni had been the one who had set it off. At one of the conferences DSP Naik held each morning to review the work of the day before he had given his dry little cough and made his suggestion. It was that, now that the cooler weather had come and tourists were beginning to arrive in numbers in Bombay, advantage should be taken of the activities of the money-exchange touts.

"Some of these foreign visitors," Nadkarni had said, "bring with them considerable sums in cash. Of course, we are all well knowing that a large proportion of this is never changed through the banks in the official manner. And we know also that the dollars, the pounds sterling and the Deutschmarks that are exchanged through the touts all become at once black money."

"Yes, yes," Inspector Radwan had broken in, speaking with an easy assurance that whatever he had to say was worth hearing. "Yes, indeed. I have already seen those fellows operating by the dozen. I could catch you one within ten minutes of leaving this office."

Was there too much confidence there, Ghote asked himself. It was a variant of the question he had encouraged his darting clawing mind to put after any one of the Bats had said anything. Was it exactly right? Or did it betray something tiny that should not be there? Was Rohit Radwan not simply confident, but putting on an air of confidence? An air of confidence designed to conceal something?

Was Radwan, after all, the man who was selling out to seths?

Ghote looked long and hard at the straight-backed, square-shouldered figure of the Muslim with that damned, shiny, glossy beard. And why, why, did a picture at once flash upon his mind of his own Protima, elegant, quick, fine-featured, and loved since the first month of their marriage?

The fight was not one where there were rests between rounds. Blows could land at any time.

"Ah, Inspector Radwan, that is all very well."

It was Kelkar, pouncing neatly in his accustomed manner. Nothing to suspect in that.

"No, Inspector, that is all very well, but if you spotted one of those fellows changing money, could you then follow him until he hands over that money to the next man in the chain? I wonder if you could. They are devilishly smart those boys."

Yes, Kelkar had as usual gone straight to the point. Easy enough to spot a money-changing tout at work. Not hard even to put a hand firmly on his shoulder at the moment the transaction finished. But to keep on the tail of a man like that, a man with a mind alive with supersensitive suspicions, that would be by no means so easy.

"Yes," Inspector Nadkarni added, "to follow a tout without arousing his suspicions, none of us would find that a simple task. However, those touts are after all only men. And men make mistakes. I propose that we go on following as many of those fellows as we can until one of them is one day careless."

So, not without reluctance to embark on such a necessarily long-drawn process, Inspector Nadkarni's plan had been adopted.

And, at last and at last, one cool Sunday evening towards the end of January a tout was careless.

It happened to Ghote at Apollo Bunder. He had been on duty there for some three hours, keeping an eye out for a tout approaching a wondering, slightly apprehensive tourist, watching for the earnest pleading and the subsequent furtive hustling of notes from hand to hand. He had managed to witness six or seven of such scenes. But either he had been too distant for there to be any hope of following the tout afterwards or something had alerted the man he had begun to trail. And what happened was all too easy among the dense throng of evening strollers.

For a few moments Ghote's watch had slackened. He had been distracted by a monkey-man, a rough country fellow wearing no more than a checked dhoti, who made a living from a pair of monkeys trained to perform simple tricks. One of the two little hunched creatures was going through a pretence of not wanting to do its next trick. Ghote knew that this too was a trick, a simple trick piled on another simple trick. But the spectacle appealed to something in him, perhaps because of the very innocence of its trickery, and in watching it for a little he forgot everything else.

The tiny man-like monkey sat in a man-like sulk, refusing to do what its duty was. A light wave of giggly laughter ran round the part of the great evening crowd ringing the monkey-man and his beasts. Ghote, at the edge of the circle, was unable to help himself joining in like a child.

Then, right at his back, he heard, gradually penetrating, a quiet pointed conversation. And it was between a pressing money tout and a cautious tourist, an American to judge by the accent of his English.

Very slowly Ghote lowered his head and twisted it round. At last out of the corner of his eye he was able to get a glimpse of the two talkers.

The American was just what a tourist ought to be. He was a big man with a cheerful red face and he was wearing a bright pink cotton tartan jacket. Already he was clutching his fat glistening leather wallet. The tout was a tall gaunt-faced man in a greasy, flapping, European-style suit. He ought to have been the holder of some not very well paid but highly respectable post, a confidential bookkeeper or the manager of a jeweller's shop. But what he really was was given away completely by the tone of his voice as Ghote heard it quietly cutting into the crowd-murmurous night air. It was a voice like a thin blade, poking and worming without cease and resolved with metal hardness to get its way. The tourist, feeling obliged to be suspicious in this exotic land, but only surface-obliged, had fallen victim to it as inevitably as the cheap look succumbs to the determined thief's levering tool.

Ghote, all alertness now, as indifferent to the antics of the little chained sulking monkey as if it had totally ceased to exist, was assessing the probabilities as fast as he could go. In two minutes more at the outside the tout would have quietly slid into the inner pocket of that greasy European jacket a bundle of crisp green dollar bills. The American would, wonderingly, be filling his shiny wallet with many more big strange rupee notes, dirty and torn and curiously smelling from the spices in the storage jars where so many of them were kept hidden. Then the chase would begin. It was vital to work out what escape routes there were through the mass of strollers, where it was light and where darkest, what objects might blot out his view as a pursuer.

But the details of his own pursuit of the man who might lead eventually to a big black-money seth were not the most urgent of Ghote's preoccupations. Taking insistent priority over everything else was the question of summoning help from his fellow Bats.

As always on this duty now, Ghote had in the pocket of his jacket a small radio transmitter. Whatever the Bats wanted in the way of up-to-date equipment they had been able to get, almost without questions asked. At this moment both Inspector Nadkarni and Inspector Kelkar were also somewhere among the crowd of tourists and strollers. He had only to slip the slim grey box out of his pocket, press the transmit button and grate the nail of his thumb across the plastic bars protecting the microphone. The rasping this would produce in the receiving sets would at once alert the other two. Then, holding the little grey plastic box close to his mouth, it would be his duty to put the pair of them fully in the picture.

It was the method Inspector Nadkarni had devised. It was calculated to make any chance pursuit into something really effective. But it also would bring all the Bats in on any lead that came up.

And it was this that Ghote was decidedly reluctant to do. If, he thought, he could track this fellow just at his back now on his own, then he alone would be in possession of the facts about him. And then he could dole them out as he wanted. To one of his colleagues at a time. So, if betrayal came, he would with any luck know at just what point in the process it had occurred. Who had been the one to know.

Yet to shadow a suspect entirely on one's own was simply asking for failure. To escape, the target would not even have to become aware that he was being followed. Chance could easily do it. A stream of fast-moving traffic just when the suspect crossed a road. A building with more than one way out. Anything, and as good a hope as the Bats had had in all the weeks they had been working on this line would be lost.

And, yes, the exchange had been decided on. The American had suddenly thrust forward a bundle of green bills.

With a tiny contraction of the muscles of his throat, Ghote plunged for taking the risk.

He made up his mind only just in time. Ten seconds later they were off. While the pink-jacketed American stood there, legs wide apart, stuffing the big, dirty, spice-scented notes into his wallet, the tout slipped cleanly away. Despite his height, he merged in a moment into the drifting mass of strollers. Had the American, suddenly prey to doubts, wanted to go back on the deal, he would have found his acquaintance of a few seconds before nowhere to be seen.

But Ghote had taken in the tiny, swift, preparatory glance the tout had given before making his move, the quick sly look. And he had at once moved off in the direction which it had indicated so as to be in motion before his quarry.

He contrived during the next two or three minutes to keep exactly the same distance between them. It was not easy. The tout was setting a pace that was surprisingly fast when to all appearances he was merely drifting along in the same dreamy way as the married couples all round sedately taking the evening air or the pairs of men friends strolling hand in hand, idly chatting and laughing.

Soon Ghote had attuned himself to the point where he could pick out that tall bony body swathed in the flapping suit from among all the others nearby without the need to let his glance rest in its direction at all. And it was as well, he thought, that he had. Because it was plain that the fellow was taking every precaution against being followed. Every now and again there would come the apparently idle glance round, first to the left, then to the right. Unless you were expecting such signs of alert attention, they would have hardly been noticeable. But they were there. It was a jungle beast he was pursuing, a hypersensitive creature.

In a minute more Ghote decided that he had better alter his station. Those regular backward glances would have noted his face among the dozens of others making their way along Strand Road at slightly differing speeds. No harm if he had appeared in those mental photographs twice or even three times. But dangerous if he was to form a tiny similar pattern in them more often than that.

And, once the fellow got it into his head that there was a chance even that he was being followed, it would be so easy for him to take evasive action. A slight increase in pace, taking advantage of some area of deeper shadow to change direction: that would be all that was needed.

What the fellow would not be able to throw off easily would be a concerted operation by at least three people practised in the art of shadowing. By himself, Inspector Kelkar and Inspector Nadkarni. But that he had rejected.

So, a little worried that his manoeuvre was bound to put the tout rather farther ahead than was strictly safe, Ghote nevertheless altered his position till he was close to the slogan-daubed sea wall. As soon as he had got himself to this point, slipping easily between the languid bodies of the strollers, he checked to make sure the familiar bony figure was where it ought to be.

It was nowhere to be seen.

Cold panic gripped Ghote at once. Fool, fool, fool, he hissed at himself.

But it was not a time for recrimination. Time instead to think. To work it out. Had the fellow spotted him? If he had, then it was more than likely he had taken action and put himself out of reach once and for all. A sudden rapid spurt, sliding between the lazily moving idlers in the way he himself had just done. It would be all that was necessary.

But if he had not been spotted? And really he ought not to have been. He had been taking every precaution. He had countered in advance every suspicion. So it might simply be that the fellow had some valid reason to have hurried on. Perhaps he had decided he had behaved like a stroller long enough and could afford to go directly now to wherever he was making for.

So, quick. Get through the crowd fast too. Keep a sharp eye out. Be ready in an instant to drop again into the role of idler.

Ghote pressed rapidly through the people in front. Systematically he sent his gaze moving ahead in much the way he had done on anti-pickpocket patrol. Only with a different purpose now. Now it was not a matter of picking out the pattern of boys or men advancing against a crowd: now it was simply a question of seeing that silhouette which was stamped on his mind.

And, ridiculous, there it was. There the fellow was after all. He must simply have hurried on a bit. And now, equally simply, he had halted for a moment. He was standing under the orangey light of a tall street lamp and peering at a small sheet of paper he had taken from his pocket.

But it had nearly been too late. The tout pushed the scrap of paper back into the side pocket of his flapping suit and moved off again. And, yes, he was going now at a much quicker pace. Hurrying to a destination.

Ghote felt a knife-sharp happiness. He was about to discover just where a tout who had exchanged a fat sum in dollars was making for. Almost beyond doubt it would be either to his own home or to somewhere where he would hand over his newly gotten hoard of black money. Either answer would be excellent. Either would put into his own hands a piece of vital information. A piece of information to be doled out later as he and he alone judged best. A supply of thick orange dye to attach to whichever suspect among the Bats he chose.

Making his way through the crowd at the same faster pace as the tall tout, Ghote resolutely refused to let himself think just who those suspects in the Bats were. To condemn one of three people to whom he felt linked by chain-strong ties: How would he be able to do it? But detecting a superior officer whose unmasking would be a fearful blow to the police service that was his own life: that would be almost as bad. Only one of them, confident, quick, and brazen Inspector Radwan, could he at all contemplate as the man he had been set to smell out.

Now that the tout was moving at this greater speed Ghote felt it was safe to keep his eyes constantly on the gaunt head above the tall body. Happily he pursued him.

And lost him.

It happened very much in one of the ways he had forecast to himself earlier. They had turned inland at the end of Strand Road and were making their way at the same rapid pace along towards the big main thoroughfare of Colaba Causeway. The tout had crossed over to the far side when they had come to the turn by the Radio Club. But Ghote had decided not to go over in his wake. He could keep him quite easily in view across the roadway and there was not likely to be much traffic at this hour. Being separated from his quarry in this way would, he had reasoned, neatly deal with any suspicions the fellow might still develop.

But the slightly unexpected had happened. There was some traffic. A procession of three vans from a chair-hire firm came up, perhaps from the Radio Club itself. They were nose-to-tail and moving slowly because pedestrians were crossing from one side to the other in an idle fashion. Ghote had considered crossing himself so as to keep the tout in view during the time the vans would come between the two of them. But he had decided to play safe and keep to the opposite side. And when the three vans had ceased to cut off his view the tall tout had disappeared.

This time Ghote fought down the panic at once. The fellow must be somewhere about. He must have stopped again to consult that scrap of paper.

He peered hard at the far side of the roadway. But nowhere, forwards or back, could he see the distinctive silhouette. He ran over and made a quick foray up towards Colaba Causeway. But he had no success. He turned and scanned the faces of the vaguely drifting idlers coming up towards him. Not a sign.

Down deep inside there was a time bomb of depression waiting to explode, the stored force of his real enemy. He pushed hard to smother it. If once he let it go, he knew that his mind would instantly be swamped with useless and fantastic ideas. Bad recriminations, ridiculous dark thoughts about the fellow's vanishing being somehow connected with Inspector Kelkar or Inspector Nadkarni. Anything. Everything.

But it must not be like that. He must think and think hard.

He stopped where he was and asked himself systematically just what he knew about the tout. Was there anything he had observed that might give him a clue? It did not, at the speed he had made his mind work, take long to hit on a lead.

The scrap of paper the fellow had consulted under the orangey lamplight. An address. It must be. What else would he need to read there and then? And if it was an address, then it must be somewhere not far away. Otherwise the fellow would have waited to read it. And if he was making for an address not far from this spot, then it would be almost certainly somewhere off Colaba Causeway.

No sooner had this thought-process zipped its way through his forcedly lucid mind than Ghote had darted into the roadway and, careless of possible traffic, had run as hard as he could go up towards the junction some three hundred yards away.

He made no attempt to spot the tout among the evening drifters on either pavement. All he had to do was to get to the head of the road as fast as he could. Then it would just be a matter of hoping that his quarry had not been running too. And, provided that he had not, he would be there at the junction before him. All he would have to do then would be to wait.

And, barely had he arrived, panting desperately, when he saw the familiar tall form coming towards him. At once he realised what must have happened.

The fellow was on the wrong side of the road. He must have, for some reason or none, slowed his pace just as those three chair-hire vans had come between them. And then when the vans had passed he had crossed over in their wake, perhaps only a yard or two behind him himself. Quite simple. Nothing at all to justify those ridiculous ideas that had so nearly broken loose in his head. No Inspector Nadkarni coming to warn the fellow in some altogether mysterious way. No Inspector Kelkar guessing by the sheer power of his will what was happening and heading off the suspect. Just a simple mistake.

In an instant Ghote came to a decision. He slipped the grey plastic two-way radio from his pocket, pressed the transmit button and ran his thumbnail across the serrations on top of the microphone. Then he told his alerted colleagues just what the situation was.

He was done with cunning. Best just to call up all the help he could and track this fellow with the black money in his pocket to wherever it was he was going.

As it turned out, help was hardly necessary. True, Inspector Kelkar did arrive, on a motor scooter he had typically had standing by, shortly before the tall tout plunged for some ten minutes into a house not far back from Colaba Causeway. But Ghote calculated that he himself could have managed the whole business perfectly well.

However, it was too late to worry about what might have been. As it was, they had an address. The address to which a considerable sum of black money had been taken. Ghote hoped in a freshwood blaze of optimism that this time there would be no hollow prize at the end of the trail.

But he feared that the bright fire would all too soon die down into sour ashes.

Inspector Nadkarni laid the trap at the Colaba address Ghote and Inspector Kelkar had found. It was a miracle of complexity.

It hinged on a ruse which Ghote found himself shaking his head over in admiration for days after he had heard Nadkarni explain it. It was simply to have DSP Naik drop a hint to one of his opposite numbers in the uniform branch that a current outbreak of car stealing was all being masterminded from the flat in Colaba. The uniform branch then either with its own resources or with the aid of men from the regular CID would keep a watch on the flat and its occupant, the syndicate agent the tall tout had visited. Such a watch would, of course, mean reports being made. Reports would, naturally, be filed. And Nadkarni was confident that he could, with the discreet passing of a few rupees in dash here and the firm use of influence there, gain nightly access to those files. Consequently the Bats' work would be done for them, with no one but Nadkarni himself knowing the results.

Well, Ghote thought to himself, at least this will mean there can be no leakage of information. If the scheme worked, Nadkarni would eventually have the address of some premises somewhere to raid. With any luck this would be the address of the seth whom the agent they were having watched would go to. Then some or all of the rest of the Bats would have to be told. And then there would be only the minimum of time for whichever one of them it was to pass on the tip to his underworld contact and for this contact to find out in the maze of rumour among the criminal element in the city where to sell the information. Clever, clever Inspector Nadkarni.

At once, automatically as pressing down a switch brings on a light, the thought rose: a man as clever as that, would he not be the best player of them all at the double-crossing game?

But, whatever game Inspector Nadkarni was playing, if he was playing a game at all, his patience did reap its reward. Ghote heard about it without realising what it was he was learning, so close to his chest was his old mentor playing his cards.

It happened at his home. He had come in very late after one of his meetings with Mr. Rao, held outside the Paradise Cinema up in Mahim. And, perhaps because once again he had had nothing to say and Mr. Rao, seeming more than a little uncomfortable in those commonplace surroundings, had been rather curt, he had been in a distinctly edgy state of temper.

Protima had attacked him for being so late and never having any attention to spare for her. And he had at once retorted that even when he was at home these days she seemed to have more attention for other people than for him.

"Other people? What other people is it?"

"Very well. It is Rohit Radwan, since you are asking."

He had not wanted to say it. He had not wanted to mix it in the unequal struggle he constantly fought. But the thought had appeared at the edge of his mind, and once it was there the temptation had been heady. To utter it would be to bring all those concealed feelings out into the open. But what if he then found they were true? Yet to be rid of those dark thoughts that he had hardly dared even to think . . .

But the great challenge had gone unnoticed. The antagonist, as if knowing that time was on his side, had moved back.

"Rohit," was all that Protima had replied, "well, there is someone who can at least make time to see his wife."

"What are you meaning?"

"Ha, he is going to be away all one night soon. He told me. He is going to Mahableshwar to visit that poor creature."

Extreme mortification had assailed Ghote then. How typical of Radwan to get time off when all the rest of them were working day and night seven days a week. No doubt he had simply gone to DSP Naik and asked, with that white-teethed smile of his shining out of that damned curly beard. No doubt, as usual, he had asked and got.

It was not until a day or two later, at the end of the month, on February the twenty-eighth itself, that he had found out that Radwan had not got time off to go to Mahableshwar after all. He had not even asked for it. What had happened was that he had been told in confidence by Inspector Nadkarni that there was to be action of some sort on February the twenty-eighth. And, no doubt in order to cover up, he had allowed Protima to believe he was going up into the hills then.

But what arrangement had he been making with Protima that he had needed to produce this story?

Ghote wished he could stop and work out every implication. But he had found out about Radwan only when Inspector Nadkarni had warned him for evening duty that February the twenty-eighth. Apparently Dayabhai Patel had reported that he was suffering another attack of stomach trouble and would not be fit. So he himself had been summoned in Dayabhai's place, and he dared not think of anything else but the action ahead now.

It seemed that what had emerged from old Nadkarni's devious plan was that the agent in the Colaba flat had visited on January the thirty-first a certain luxury house whose exact location Nadkarni was still keeping to himself. The visit had been made in great stealth and was almost certainly the time when the agent's accumulation of black money had been handed over. And what happened on the last day of one month was likely to happen, Nadkarni had reckoned, on the last day of the next.

So a raid was to take place when the seth had at his house all the proceeds brought to him by perhaps several agents. Would it be successful? Would this time all their previous failures be blotted out? And, if they were, would that mean only that the betrayer had not for once had time to act? Ghote longed for the night that would answer these questions.

X

Ghote stood, holding himself perfectly still and forcing himself to relax, behind the thick circular trunk of the tall leaning palm that rose above him high into the night air. Fifty yards away was the outline of the beach bungalow at fashionable Juhu which Inspector Nadkarni had eventually disclosed as being the target of their operation. A persistent cool breeze coming in from the sea made Ghote want to sneeze. He was glad he was wearing a jacket and one of his better thicker pairs of trousers, one of the pairs that had become associated with his life in the high-flying Bats.

Below him he could hear the sea trickling monotonously in and out over the smooth sand. That and the tiny insistent noises of night insects were all that there was to be heard.

Certainly the others, presumably moving now into the final positions Inspector Nadkarni had allotted them, were making no sound of any sort. If they were going to find their man had gone, it would not be because of any clumsy stupidity now.

But had their man already left the so carefully surrounded house? It was possible. There could theoretically have been time to get a message to him between the moment Inspector Nadkarni had given them a name and the final setting of the trap. That, if they were to have as much information as they ought to have, had been unavoidable.

Was he gone? Or was he there still behind closely drawn curtains, having "a last peg," leaning back in a luxurious armchair, glorying in his riches and never thinking that they had been obtained, every rupee, at the expense of his fellow citizens, the ones who did pay their taxes, did not seek to buy smuggled goods, kept shops that declared every item for sales tax? And there were many people like that. More, far more, than would ever be believed by the habitually cynical, the routine doubters of every healthy-looking exterior.

In the soft and velvet darkness Ghote peered at the luminous hands of his wrist watch. One minute from midnight now. One minute to go.

He counted out the seconds. Then he began moving softly forward, his feet making no sound in the yielding sand. The details of the bungalow's exterior loomed clearer with every step. Yes, there was the door at the back that was his particular pigeon. And, yes, this should be near enough.

He waited.

With a suddenness that, despite his expecting it, gave him a start of shock there came the thunder of knocking at the front door on the other side of the building.

And then silence.

Ghote strained every fibre to hear. Steps inside the house should be audible to him here. Would they be those of a servant roused up and going sleepily but confidently to answer this late-night visitor? Or would they be the furtive movements of a man preparing to leave by the back way in a hurry?

He braced himself.

Nothing. Then another tattoo of fiery knocking from the front. And now a voice.

"Open up. Open up. Police hai. Police hai."

Hard to recognise patient old Inspector Nadkarni in those loud and authoritative tones. But they brought no answer.

"Open up. Or we break in."

Again no answer.

"All right, Radwan."

The crash of glass now as Rohit Radwan attacked a window on the far side. Ghote crouched slightly, like a hockey goalkeeper expecting a rush of forwards with the little white ball dodging in front of them. But nothing stirred in his field of view.

Soon he heard noises from inside the house, coarse and confident. It would be Radwan going through the rooms, conducting a sharp but totally thorough search.

But this time his confidence would not be rewarded. Ghote knew it in his bones.

"Inspector Nadkarni. Not a bloody soul."

Yes. Empty. The carefully surrounded trap and nothing in it. The beast warned. But who by? Who by?

Before long, however, Ghote was to get some way towards having an answer to that question.

But it was not until well into the next day that he could even be perfectly certain that the question had to be asked. It might be possible, he had told himself that night, that the seth had simply taken it into his head to go somewhere else. But when inquiries revealed that their man had left for Delhi by car at much the time that they had been setting out for Juhu from Bombay itself and that in Delhi no one of his name was known, then it was impossible to cling to the optimistic view any longer.

It was at this point that Ghote's difficulties began. He needed to know whether Inspector Nadkarni had confided the address of the Juhu bungalow to anybody at all before he had given them that final briefing. DSP Naik had not been present at the briefing, but had he already been told the address? Or had Nadkarni perhaps consulted with Inspector Kelkar before giving the rest of them their final orders? Had he needed to tell anyone outside the Bats so as to obtain equipment of some sort?

Ghote had to find out. And eventually he hit on a ruse for doing so.

Another lie, he noted when at last an opportunity arose to speak to Inspector Nadkarni in private. Another lie to add to the precarious scaffolding of ever-thinning bamboo lengths that, crazily knotted, he was building higher and higher above the firm foundations of original truth. But this was a lie that had to be told. He must weave its consequences into the fabric of his life as best he might.

"Inspector," he said to Nadkarni, going across to the door of the now vacated Bats office and making sure that it was shut. "Inspector, there is something weighing on my conscience that I would like to tell."

Nadkarni, perched hoveringly over some papers as usual, looked up at him through the familiar gold-edged spectacles.

"Inspector?" he said.

"It is something concerned with the security of the Juhu operation," Ghote blurted out, almost wanting to vanish as soon as the words were said.

Nadkarni gave his little dry cough.

"By all means tell, Inspector," he said. "But first ask something of yourself."

"Ask something?"

"Yes, my dear fellow. Ask whether, when you have told, you will be as happy as you now think you would be."

Oh, Inspector Nadkarni, Inspector Nadkarni, Ghote thought, I still have so much to learn from you. Who else would be so strong-minded that they would push away a rich offering like this? Who else would deliberately delay the moment of learning perhaps who the betrayer of the Bats was?

He let a few moments of silence go by.

"No, Inspector," he said at last. "I wish to tell you this whatever the consequences."

"Well, if you are determined to be reckless, I see that nothing I say would stop you. Go on, my dear fellow."

"Inspector, I broke security before we set off for Juhu last night."

"Yes?" Nadkarni said quietly.

"It was like this," Ghote went on, wondering fiercely whether the coming lie would do what he hoped. "I have been very worried recently concerning my wife. Concerning her attitude towards me. I have the feeling that, quite suddenly, she has begun to leave me altogether out of account."

He hated himself as he spoke. To use the truth to tell his lie. The truth that he had not dared to put into words before, even in his mind. The truth about his most private world. Where was he going?

He felt bruised and battered almost to dropping-point. But he pushed himself on.

"So," he continued, looking straight into the assessing eyes from which the gold-rimmed spectacles had been slowly removed, "so above all I wished her to know for certain where I was after office hours. I did not wish to give her reasons from my side for having doubts."

"And so you telephoned her and told her you would be going out to Juhu last night? And that the business was arranged for midnight exactly?"

"Inspector, it is worse. Inspector, I told her all the details. The name, the exact address, everything."

"Yes," Nadkarni said with a quiet sigh. "I suppose it was that you wished to place on her a burden of trust. Is that it?"

"Yes. Yes, it was that."

Ghote recorded with awe the way Nadkarni could see into his mind. He had not done what the old inspector had suggested. But he knew that, given the circumstances, that was exactly what he would have done.

Nadkarni gave his little cough now.

"So what we have to ask ourselves," he said, "is whether Mrs. Ghote has access to criminal circles through which she could pass on her information."

"Sir," Ghote said, dropping back to the mode of address he had used when he was raw in the CID. "Sir, I do not believe that she can have such access. Certainly, there is no one that I know of. But on the other hand, sir, if it is physically impossible for a warning to have been passed by anybody else, then, sir, I must believe the worst."

He forced himself to assume an expression of grey heaving woe. Or, he acknowledged, there was no need to force such a feeling. Only to hold it hard and to forget its origin. He certainly felt woeful enough. But it was sorrow for having to cheat of all people, Nadkarni, that was heavy in him. His doubts about Protima were false. Surely they were false for all that they jabbed so. Surely.

Inspector Nadkarni regarded him steadily and in silence. He positively felt the truth of the whole matter being dragged up to the surface of his mind. And there it would be reflected, plain as plain, on his features. He dug his heels in against the tugging, shut his eyes (though keeping them steadfastly open) and resisted.

And at last Nadkarni broke his silence.

"Yes, my dear fellow, I see what you mean. And I think . . ."
He paused.

Would he agree to divulge his secrets? Would he?

"Yes, my dear chap, I think it would be right to tell you all I know."

It was done. But those words "I think it would be right" pierced Ghote to the core. To trade on the ultimate feelings of rightness that had made Nadkarni, surely, what he was: it was miserably despicable.

But he expressed his thanks. He even contrived to make his voice break a little with emotion as he did so. And then he sat back and sucked in the information that he had lied and cheated to get.

No, DSP Naik, for one, had never been told who the Bats were hoping to arrest out at Juhu. He had delegated full responsibility for the whole affair. And neither had Dayabhai Patel ever learnt the name, though he had known before his attack of stomach trouble that the night of February the twenty-eighth had to be kept free. He had even appeared in the office just after the final briefing had ended "in case after all he was wanted." But he had looked so washed-out that Nadkarni had sent him straight home to bed.

So that left only four of them. Inspector Kelkar, Inspector Radwan, Ghote, and Inspector Nadkarni himself. Four people only who knew the name and the address.

Could there have been a leak anywhere else? Nadkarni had considered the possibility.

"We are dealing with human beings, my dear fellow. There cannot ultimately be any question of saying that we have got an absolutely watertight system. There is always the chance, the remote chance, for instance, that someone else contrived to look at those reports in the uniform branch files in the same manner as I did. But it is not exactly a likely contingency."

Nadkarni gave his little dry cough.

It was the black cap of old on the judge's wigged head. It was the thumbs-down of the Roman Emperor from the yellowed pages of the school history primer. No appeal was practicable. One of the four of them must be guilty.

Four names. Which meant, for him, only three possibilities. Inspector Radwan, the man he would like it to be, the smiling fellow he would love to see knocked off his perch and yet someone, he feared, who was only confident on that perch because he was truly secure there. Or Inspector Kelkar, the man he admired with all his heart for possessing, simply and abundantly, that never-quailing punchiness in face of whatever opposition life placed in his path, a quality which he himself had come at length to value, tried indeed to reach and even sometimes in small measure achieved. Or

Inspector Nadkarni himself, at this very moment showing at an unguessed best those very characteristics that he had striven to implant in his own mind from his earliest beginnings as a detective. Nadkarni. Or Kelkar. Kelkar or Nadkarni.

Or could it not, please, be Radwan?

"Well, my dear fellow, no use in blinking the facts," Nadkarni went on, his voice no louder or more emphatic than usual. "So far as I have been able to reconstruct events after I had told the three of you—and, naturally, I was keeping a pretty sharp eye out—there were opportunities for each one of you to get to a telephone. They were short opportunities, but they were there. And I cannot see that there could have been any other way of passing on a message quickly enough than per telephone."

"Any one of the three of us?" Ghote echoed bleakly.

He too had been keeping a sharp eye out from that moment the night before that Nadkarni had put them in possession of such valuable information. And he had now a growing suspicion that he was in a position to correct his old mentor's assumption. But he let him have out his say. Perhaps it would reveal something to lighten the dilemma ahead.

"Yes," Nadkarni answered. "Kelkar went down ahead of me to get the car. I had intended to go with him, but you know his somewhat impulsive way. Young Patel had just come in with his request to volunteer and I had to have my word with him. By then Kelkar had rushed off, and I still had to lock up here. Naturally I could not leave the office in an insecure state. And that was when Radwan and you yourself, my dear chap, also got out of my sight for a few minutes. I presume, indeed, that was when you telephoned your wife."

"Yes. Yes, it was."

Ghote realised, with mixed feelings of pleasure and self-disgust, the considerable time he had spent working out when he could have made such a call before he had launched on his invented story had paid dividends.

Nadkarni shook his head sadly.

"I take responsibility," he said. "I ought to have contrived matters so that no one was ever out of sight once I had passed on the name and address. But the time that you all were away from me was certainly very short. It entailed taking a hell of a risk."

Two black thoughts arose now simultaneously in Ghote's mind. One was that, looked at from the twisted topsy-turvy point-of-view that he had nowadays to force himself to bring to everything, Nadkarni might not really be blaming himself at this minute. He might instead be secretly congratulating himself for having neatly engineered the situation in which the three of them had each had an opportunity to get to a telephone. If any one of them was in a position to have passed on the warning, then a much-earlier tip-off from Nadkarni himself would be brilliantly concealed. The second black thought was that, in fact, only one of the three of them had actually been left on his own. Inspector Kelkar.

Because, unknown to Nadkarni, Radwan had lingered at the first landing below the Bats office when they had left after the briefing. He had lingered in order to talk to him himself.

The whole episode came to his mind now with film-like clarity. Radwan had gone out of the office looking almost as keenly ready for the fray as Kelkar himself, eyes flashing, shoulders back, tall and confident. And a few moments later he himself had left, wondering whether to stay on while old Nadkarni locked up and double-checked but too concerned to keep a watch over the others to wait. So he had hurried out and down the broad stairway, cold in the night chill, and to his surprise he had found Radwan waiting on the first landing.

"Ah, Ganesh, my friend."

"Oh. Hello."

He could not bring himself to call the fellow Rohit.

"Well, Ganeshji, so we are both to be together on this tamasha."

"Yes. But I do not think that it ought to be considered in the light of a noisy entertainment. The greatest secrecy will be necessary."

And Radwan had laughed. Standing there on the landing throwing back his head, letting the white teeth flash deep in that glossy beard, he had laughed.

"Oh, my good Ganesh. Always so serious. Let me tell you, man, you will not go far in this life if you do not take things with a laugh."

Then what could only be described as a malicious twinkle had come into the fellow's eyes.

"Yes," he had gone on, giving him one of those hearty slaps

on the back he so much detested. "Yes, my dear chap, that is what you should learn to do. To laugh. It is what gets you places. In our sort of work. In anything. And especially with the women. Eh? Eh?"

"I have been assured that is the case, yes."

"But it is so. I know. I have proved it over and over again. I prove it nearly every day even now."

And he had stood calmly looking down, with his eyes still full of that accursed twinkling. As if he could actually see what was passing through his own mind, the had-to-be-asked question "With what woman have you been proving that nearly every day?"

At last he himself had managed to break the tingling transmissive silence between them, to back away from the rain of silent stinging blows.

"Inspector Kelkar will have the vehicle ready."

And they had gone down the remainder of the stairs together and had waited for a minute or so until Kelkar had turned up with the car. So there had been no time for Radwan to have got to a telephone.

So it could not be him. So it must lie now, it must, between Kelkar, who alone had had the opportunity of sending out a quick message after they had been given the Juhu address, and Nadkarni, who had not needed that opportunity. Nadkarni or Kelkar. Kelkar or Nadkarni.

XI

Nadkarni or Kelkar. Ghote, convinced that he had at least narrowed the unpleasant possibilities of his task in the Bats to this thought-annihilating balance, could not in the days that followed find any way of resolving it one way or the other. The scales were weighed equally down on both sides.

Nor did presenting his findings to Mr. Rao help. They met inside the General Post Office with its long clamouring queues and the dense resistant clerkly calm on the far side of the counters. Quickly and quietly in a remote corner Ghote told Mr. Rao exactly to what point his thoughts had led. He had hoped for an irrefutable explanation of why what he had said could not be so. None came. Mr. Rao did add that nothing in the inquiries he had had made into both men's private circumstances had so far shown anything suspicious, but otherwise he produced nothing to challenge Ghote's bleak assumption. What he did do was to instruct him with a shark's fin touch of unusual fierceness "to get it over and done with, and quickly." And then, as if appalled to have raised his voice, even if ever so slightly, he had glanced rapidly all round the huge crowded and noisy interior of the great building. And at once they had parted.

Ghote had gone home feeling even more depressed than he had been already. And, of course, he had quarrelled with Protima again.

This time it had not been remotely her fault. The fact was, he later acknowledged to himself though he could not acknowledge it to her, that the state of suspiciousness in which he now always worked had seeped like a bile-yellow gas into all the dealings of every part of his life. He was embroiled with it fully now. It was a sheer slogging match, and he had begun to feel that all he could do was grimly to back away from every clinch.

But he found he was incapable of thinking other than dark thoughts about his wife. She was guilty. He knew it. She was guilty of something with Radwan. What exactly it was he still refused to let himself contemplate. But it was something, something. What might not have happened during some period in those many hours when he had been away from home? And when Radwan, because of the often alternating times of their duties, was there in that house over the way? There. An enforced bachelor. A man with plenty of excuses to come begging assistance over this or that aspect of his housekeeping. Begging assistance from a kindly neighbour.

What was it he had said? Laughing a lot: it "got you places" with women. And he had claimed he was proving that nearly every day.

Who with? Who with?

A rain of damaging blows went home.

And then, about a fortnight after the Juhu washout had posed that unanswerable either-or, the bile-sharp tide took a sudden swirling lunge forward over a whole new area of the dry sands of Ghote's existence. It swirled forward and enveloped, of all people, his little Ved.

A tiny thing released the sweeping flood: a cricket fee. Ved played for a team made up of boys of his age from Government Quarters No 4, and their fee for the season had been fixed at Rupees 1.10. Ghote had had no qualms about giving Ved that sum when he had asked for it. Indeed, he had felt a certain pride at this small drain on his resources. But then, on that fatal day, Ved came to him and confessed that he had not handed over the money.

"Some rotten fellow took it from my pocket," he said, giving a defiant stare.

Ghote at once was as busy with suspicions as a nest of wasps. He jumped to his feet and stood leaning tensely over Ved.

"But it is long past the time when the fee was to be paid," he snapped. "You have had that money for weeks. How can you come to me now and say that you have not paid?"

Ved swallowed.

"Pitaji, I did not dare to tell."

"Not dare? Not dare? What excuse is that? How could you not dare to tell—if the money was taken from your pocket?"

"But it was. It was."

Ved's eyes slowly turned away. Ghote's suspicions swirled up and whined anew.

"You say it was taken by some rotten fellow?" he pounced. "Very well, what is the name of this fellow? He will be caught and punished, I promise you. I am not police officer for nothing."

"Pitaji, if I had known it I would have told."

"Now you are saying that you do not know. One minute ago only it was exactly the opposite you were saying."

"No, Pitaji."

"Yes, I say. Yes. Oh, one thing is evident to me. You are telling a pack of lies altogether. Yes. And I mean to get to the bottom of them, pretty damn quick."

At this point Protima appeared.

"What is this? What is this? What for are you shouting? What are you asking the boy?"

Ghote felt a great flame of rage whoosh up. What was she doing interfering? If he was to get to the bottom of the business, it was most important he did not lose his grip on Ved. He had him running. He must not be side-tracked.

"Answer me, boy," he thundered, though at some place in the side of his mind he was aware that his question was not altogether logical and that his thunder was louder than the case merited. "Answer me."

Tears appeared suddenly in Ved's eyes as he brought them reluctantly to look at his father.

"But it is nothing, Pitaji," he said incoherently. "Nothing."

"Nothing? What are you meaning 'Nothing'? Come, I want answer. I want answer."

"But how can the boy answer?" Protima came boring in, persistent as a mosquito. "How can he answer when you are not telling him what is the question?"

"No," Ghote shouted, swinging round to her in blind exasperation. "No. Get out. Go away. Leave us."

"I will not leave. Not when you are shouting at the boy in this way."

An icy, and totally spurious, calm gripped Ghote.

"Very well," he said. "I will not shout at the boy. Now, will you go?"

"No. Not until I am knowing thoroughly what is all this nonsense."

"Nonsense? Nonsense? Is it nonsense when your son turns into a thief?"

"But, Pitaji—"

"Silence," Ghote bellowed. "Silence. How can you deny that you are a thief? You come to me now and say that you have not paid your cricket fee, and I was giving you the money months ago. How can you deny?"

"But, Pitaji, Pitaji, it was not months. Pitaji, I am knowing the date. Because Captain was telling us that by—"

"No. I will not have this."

Ghote swung round on Protima.

"You see what your son has come to? Lies, lies, lies. He has spent his cricket fee on sweetmeats of all descriptions, and now he is hoping that I will again pay. He thinks he has found a way of making easy living for life. Soon he will be deciding that he can steal with impunity from all and sundry. He will end up in a pickpocketing gang."

"But, Pitaji, Pitaji," Ved shouted back, "I was not stealing. It was that rotten fellow who was stealing from us."

"Now we are back to that," Ghote stormed in return. "Now we are back to—"

"But if the boy had his fee stolen," Protima interrupted, in a tone that seemed to seek to bring some reasonableness into the situation.

Ghote turned to her with joyful savagery. Whatever else he did, he was determined, he would at least take a directly contrary view to anything said by this woman who was betraying him.

"But he did not have his fee stolen," he pronounced. "He wasted every paise of it on sweetmeats. And now he will be punished. Not one single coin will he get out of me. Let him resign from team. Let him resign and play cricket in the street. That will teach him."

At this Ved burst into wail upon wail of appalling loudness.

"Stop that noise, stop that noise," Ghote commanded. "You will be having every neighbour thinking we are beating you. Stop it at once."

To his surprise, and even a little to his chagrin, Ved did stop. With complete abruptness.

A great vacuum was left. All three of them stood, as it were, on the edge of it and looked at each other, exhausted and fearful.

At last Ghote spoke.

"I will not pay that fee again," he said, in a voice trembling with the effects of emotional excess. "I will not pay."

And he turned at once and walked quickly out of the house before anyone else could say anything that would set them all off again. He felt appalling, a boxer gasping for breath, purple with bruises, cut about and down on his knees.

For two whole days after the scene with Ved, Ghote was able to keep it out of his mind only when he was actively engaged with work. Even when, he knew, he ought to have been trying to devise some way of eliminating either Inspector Kelkar or Inspector Nadkarni from the accusation that faced them he kept finding he was thinking about Ved. The boy's face, tear-stained and suddenly silence-struck, appeared before him, swimming up like a vision.

At home not a word more was said about the cricket fee. Ved, after a day of being whisperingly subdued, seemed to be back to his usual, modestly cheerful self. But Ghote knew that a row as monumental as theirs would still be having its effect, lurking only a little below the surface.

He had only to judge by his own feelings. All during the day as he dutifully plodded round the treadmill of the Bats' seemingly disaster-doomed task, and in the evenings devoted to the same grind, that sad face was always looming into view. It appeared as he wearily mounted yet another stone stairway in yet another high-built chawl looking for some new recipient of money illegally sent from England. Or on tout-spotting duty out at Santa Cruz as the tourists came off the aircraft, or outside the big shops in Dadabhai Naoroji Road, rising up between himself and his objective would come the thought of Ved and of every detail and word of that sudden unexpected clash between them.

Because it had been an altogether unexpected clash. It took Ghote three days to make this admission to himself. But, once made, there could be no denying it. Ved had never been in the habit of defying his parents. He was possessed of a sweet reason-ableness. It was his most attractive quality. And he himself had not been in the habit of getting Ved to do what he had to do by shouting and threats. They had never been necessary.

So how had that fearful shouting match come about? He must have been partly to blame himself. No, he had been almost wholly to blame.

The revelation came to him as he stood on the veranda of an aging building in which it was possible that a family receiving black-money payments from England lived. In front of him was a roughly made wooden door with the hasp of its crude fastening unpadlocked. He had noted that this must mean there was some-body at home and had raised his hand to knock on the door when the thought had come. He stood there foolishly, accepting its impli-cations. Then he managed to pull himself together, gather up the scraps of information he possessed about the people he had come to see and this time bring his knuckles sharply down on the rough planks of the door. Then began once more a round of careful and cajoling questions that might or might not lead to a grudging ac-knowledgement that black-money payments were being received. From them he might or might not manage to learn the name of the person paying out. This person might or might not lead them on to a sub-agent. The sub-agent might or might not lead to an agent. The agent might, but most probably would not, lead at last to the seth of a syndicate. And then at last and at last there might come a much needed major success for the Bats. If they were not betrayed first.

If, in all probability, they were not betrayed either by Inspector Nadkarni, that model of policemanlike patience, or by Inspector Kelkar, combining in one person all the dash and vigour of a crack regiment of tanks pushing and thrusting against the enemy.

But it was late in the evening of that day, after having exhausted this and one other possibility that, going home in a bus for once empty enough for him to have secured a seat, he came to make an admission to himself altogether more far-reaching than his mere inner agreement that he and Ved did not usually quarrel.

Sitting punished with tiredness and seeing once more that vision of Ved's face shocked into silence, it came to him that right from the very start of that disastrous encounter something had been wrong. It was that, straight away, he had not accepted Ved's word.

How had he come not to realise this? It seemed now as if he had been shown some deep, time-engrained, never yet perceived truth. The fact that he had begun by believing that Ved must be telling a lie.

Of course, he told himself, it would be absurd to believe the boy never told lies. He told them as often as any other child, and as obviously. But it was equally true that he had never, if it had become a matter of importance, tried to make out that things were other than they were. This was something he knew about his son. The boy was not, when it came to fundamentals, a persistent and unrepentant liar.

So he had not, of course, of course, lied about the cricket fee. It had, of course, of course, been really taken from him by some juvenile pickpocket. And of course he had been afraid to admit that, perhaps partly owing to carelessness, he had been robbed. He had hoped, in the way children did hope, that something some-how would happen to relieve him of a too heavy burden. That was what that flick of last-minute evasiveness had been about.

And he himself ought to have known that about his own son. He had known it on other occasions. A dozen times and more in the boy's ten years there had been similar incidents when there had come into his mind the suspicion that the boy was lying, only for it to crumble at once in face of the obvious truth of things. Ved on important matters did not lie. Ved, quite often, was afraid to tell the truth.

Why had he not known this at once this time? The answer presented itself like a knock-out blow. He had not recognised the reality of the situation because for the past six months and more his mind had gradually become nothing less than a machine for suspecting.

His stop grew near as the big red double-deck bus lumbered on its journey. He pushed himself to his feet, waited till the vehicle had slowed almost to a halt and jumped neatly off. But, as the bus drew away from the stop, he stayed just where he had jumped.

Yes, certainly he would go to Ved the moment that he got home. He would wake him if he was asleep. And he would tell him as plainly and emphatically as he could that he no longer had the least doubt that that cricket fee had been taken away from him by some pickpocketing boy. But that would not be all.

Standing there alone in the enwrapping darkness, he knew that, as certainly as he was going to tell Ved not to worry any more about the cricket fee, he was also going to tell Protima that he had come to an absolute, unbreakable, teak-strong decision.

He was going to resign from the Bombay Police Force. In the unequal fight he was going to do the only thing left to him, throw in the towel.

XII

Next day, first thing in the morning, Ghote sent to Mr. Rao a signal, in a form long before agreed between them, by which he requested an urgent interview. Into Police Headquarters post-system he slipped a letter written in crude block capitals on rough paper threatening anonymously to kill the Assistant Commissioner with eighty-four stabs before midday. In the simple code they had fixed on, midday would then be the time they were to meet and the place would be No 84 on the guide map to Bombay supplied for tourists, Churchgate Station.

Ghote felt he had a duty to inform Mr. Rao as soon as possible of his decision to quit the force. If the dilemma between Inspector Nadkarni and Inspector Kelkar was to be resolved, or if by some remote chance it was to be proved that one of the other Bats was the man selling out, then a replacement for himself would have to be added to the Squad with all possible speed.

Once he had surreptitiously dropped the letter in its coarse brown envelope into the post box he felt a sense of achievement, though a somewhat dazed one. It was as if he had succeeded in pulling out a loose tooth. The thing had been done, even though the soreness remained. Something concrete had taken place to make the decision irrevocable.

Certainly that had not happened when he had told Protima the night before. She had first, of course, been astounded. Police work, that had seemed to be her husband's life for as long as they had been married, that had been her rival in his affections, that had claimed more of his time and energies than he had left her take, suddenly no longer to be there. She had been struck dumb. Indeed, beyond repeating the word "Resign," she had said nothing at all.

He had been reduced by her silence to expostulating with her. Cascadingly he had produced every argument he could lay hands on to back the decision, as if she were actually bitterly opposing him. He claimed he had been thinking of it for months, that it had only been his sudden transfer to the Bats that had delayed the moment. He said that it was the acknowledgement of his own failure within the larger failure of the Bats that had made him now take the plunge.

"Even your Rohit Radwan has not been a genius on this job," he had taunted.

At this point it had seemed that she had suddenly come to life. She had begged him to reconsider the decision, or at least put it off. Of course, so he told himself, he had at once seen through that. No doubt she had just realised that when his resignation went through they would no longer be entitled to a Government Quarters house. They would no longer be living so conveniently close to that damned, shiny-bearded, smiling Muslim.

He had said then curtly that there was nothing to discuss. His mind was made up. He would be handing in his resignation officially in the morning.

Well, he had not precisely done that. He had realised that before writing the formal letter to DSP Naik, his official superior, he had to contact Mr. Rao.

Was he giving himself a last-minute let-out, he asked as he approached the high-fronted, tall-towered Churchgate Station some ten minutes before noon. He threaded his way through the crowds hurrying up the steps even though morning and evening rush hours were far away. No, he decided, this was no let-out. There was nothing he would more delight in than some extraordinary heaven-sent event which would make it possible to continue in the life he had thought would always be his. But nothing like that would happen. He was going to resign, and that was that. Suspicion had undone him.

He looked round the busy station concourse. People in scores were scurrying this way and that to catch their trains. Others were sitting patiently waiting. Some even were lying at full length on the dusty paving stones. Coolies, red-turbaned and red-shirted, moved here and there with suitcases and boxes and fat rolls of bedding on their heads. Vendors with little handcarts or with trays suspended from their necks thrust their wares at every passer-by, bright bottles of mineral water, plaster statuettes of the gods, multicoloured film magazines, paper twists of gram and nuts. Mr. Rao, who, tall and aloof, would have stood out in any crowd, was not yet to be seen.

Methodically Ghote set about finding a suitable spot for their meeting. A narrow passageway between two high stacks of goods waiting to be loaded, boxes, crates and baskets of all sorts, seemed to be the best place. As soon as he had made sure of it he went and paraded himself as conspicuously as he could among the crowds. Above, in the roof, the dozens of huge-bladed fans swung in a wild whirl that reflected the state of his own mind.

To leave the police. The thought was too overwhelming to grasp. What would he do instead of police work? He had never for a moment before this imagined himself doing anything else. Since long before he had first signed on he had seen himself as being one of those men whom his imagination had fastened on in earliest boyhood. He had wanted to be one of the people who went about leaving behind them in the choppy chaos of the world a wake of calm. He had wanted to be a putter of things right.

A job as a security officer? It was the obvious thing to try for. There were openings of that sort for experienced policemen. Only the other day he had met a Superintendent who had been in charge out at Wardha and who was now on secondment as chief security officer for the Maharashtra State Transport Corporation. But jobs like that would be no good for him. No good at all. Their chief requirement was precisely the quality of suspicion. And he had had too much of suspicion.

Ah. Mr. Rao. There. By the booking office. Standing out above the long patient queues of people waiting to obtain tickets.

Ghote hurried across, and, as soon as he was sure Mr. Rao had seen him, led the way to the narrow gap between the two huge stacks of railway parcels. Quickly he checked that no one had come to stand or squat near enough to overhear what might be said. Then he slipped into the shadowed gap. A moment or two later Mr. Rao came up, pacing thoughtfully among the hurrying passengers. Then, with a sudden furtive dart that, even to Ghote, made him look a little ridiculous, he slipped into the hidey-hole.

"Well, man," he said at once, "you've got proof? At last?"

"Sir. Mr. Rao. No."

"No? Then what the devil have you pulled me out of my seat for?"

A hot sweat flushed through Ghote's every pore. What a terrible beginning.

"Sir," he said, "I very much regret but, sir, I am about to hand in my resignation."

"Resignation? Resignation? What the devil do you mean? What resignation?"

"Sir, from the Force."

Mr. Rao looked at him in mild astonishment.

"Do you mean to tell me, Ghote," he said, "that you are leaving the service? Why did you say nothing of this before?"

"Sir. Mr. Rao. I have only just decided."

"Only just— But surely you're not quitting because you haven't brought this business to a conclusion? Because if so, let me tell you that you've done remarkably well. Remarkably well."

Ghote could hardly believe his ears. Remarkably well. But he thought he had been doing appallingly.

"But, sir," he said.

"No, no, no. You're up against the very toughest opposition, remember. Men good enough to be drafted into the Black-money and Allied Transactions Squad are going to take a hell of a lot of catching if they turn rotten. And you've narrowed it down. But now you're trying to best an officer of the calibre of Inspector Kelkar, or of Inspector Nadkarni come to that. You're not going to bring either of them to book in ten minutes."

Ghote felt the whirling thoughts that had been in his mind ever since he had taken his great decision rise now to howling dust devils. If he had been doing as well as this, ought he not to stay on? He did not want to resign. He wanted to spend all his working life—

No. No, no, no, he thundered to himself. He did want to resign. He was out for the count. He was a creature of suspicions now. And he wanted not to be. He wanted to cast that vile yellow skin, though it had become part of his living flesh.

"Sir, please," he said. "Sir, you do not at all understand. Sir, I wish to resign because, sir, my mind has become nothing more than suspicions only. Yes, sir, that is it. I am altogether too suspicious, sir, and I will not go on."

Mr. Rao, all distinction and calm, looked down at him. Behind, a noisy family procession went by on their hurried way to one of the platforms. The father in front was shouting hoarsely that they would miss the train and dragging with him a boy of Ved's age, looking round at everything except the way he was meant to be going. Two tearful and howling little girls in bright fresh cotton frocks were being loudly chivvied and herded along by the mother, a stout lady in a dark-red sari carrying a huge handbag and a fat black umbrella. And finally there came a coolie, expostulating and back-answering under his maximum head-load of three bulging suitcases.

"Suspicion, is it, Ghote?"

Mr. Rao sounded distant and thoughtful, as if he was communing with himself in some quiet garden.

"But, my dear chap, a sense of suspicion is a very necessary quality in the successful officer. You should be pleased to possess as much of it as you do. You'd have got nowhere against Nadkarni and Kelkar without a well-developed sense of suspicion."

"But, sir. Sir, I have accused my own son of thieving even, sir."

Mr. Rao looked down calmly still.

"You let it get out of hand, did you?" he said. "Well, I can understand that. But you're not telling me you still think your son is a thief, are you?"

"No, sir. No, I do not."

"And he isn't a thief? Children do steal things, you know."

"No, sir. He is not a thief. I am satisfied now that he did not take the money that was missing. Thoroughly satisfied."

"Well, then, Ghote, I am going to ask you to change your mind about all this. I've been impressed with your work. I may as well tell you that I chose you with some misgivings. But you've proved yourself. You don't make a great show of things, but you stick at it. And that's what I like in an officer."

He looked gravely down at Ghote.

"Now," he said, "will you go back on your decision?"

Ghote nearly said Yes.

But when, in going over Mr. Rao's words, he turned his mind to Ved he found himself presented also with a picture of Protima. And looming behind her there was the smiling assured figure of

Rohit Radwan. No, he had to get her away from the influence of that fellow. He had to.

"Sir, no. Sir, I much regret. But I cannot do it, sir."

For a moment Mr. Rao's eyes took on a look of quick shrewdness. Then they went carefully and remotely blank.

"Very well, man. It's your own life. You must live it as you think best. I suppose you've taken into account pension rights and all that sort of thing?"

"Yes, sir."

He shot the lie straight out.

"And you've some idea where you can get a job that will keep you and your family at the standards you've been used to? Any other children, are there?"

"No others, sir. And, yes, I have thought about alternative employment."

And, sir, he would have liked to have added, those standards you spoke of are not so very high, sir. Cost-of-living is rising faster than pay and allowances, Mr. Rao, sir.

But that tall spare figure was not the person to whom such sharp and carping remarks could be made.

"Very well then, Ghote, I shall regard your duties under me as terminated as from now."

Mr. Rao turned. But, even at this moment, he did not leave the shelter of the tall stacks of boxes and baskets without taking a long cautious look at the people-thronged concourse. It would not do if, by some thousand-to-one unlucky chance, Inspector Nadkarni should happen to be there, or Inspector Kelkar. Even the possibility of someone mentioning to one of them that an Assistant Commissioner had been seen in close conversation with a member of the Squad might be fatal.

But at last he suddenly nipped forward and joined the mass of travellers. And once again a stooping dodginess turned his austere figure for an instant into something almost laughable.

Then, out of the stacks' shelter and even as he switched back into being a tall and distant tower, he turned and raising his voice a little he sent a few last words back to Ghote hidden in the shadows.

"Remember fire. And water. Neither of those should be let get out of hand. And if you do change your mind, it's the same signal."

And abruptly almost as if he regretted having spoken, Mr. Rao wheeled away. In a few long strides he was far off among the jostling bustle.

Ghote gave him three solid minutes by his watch to get clear of possible witnesses. He felt scoured bare. A great watery sadness slowly invaded him. He had gone past the limit now. There could be no going back, despite what Mr. Rao had called out to him. He could not bring into use that secret and elaborate signal mechanism just to say "Sir, I have made a mistake after all. I did not mean what I said." To do that would be to burn up in an instant whatever good opinion he had made for himself with Mr. Rao. It would be like touching a scrap of cigarette paper to a blazing fire.

But he had earned Mr. Rao's good opinion. For a moment, as he made his way out of the station into Vir Nariman Road, he hugged the thought hard.

Then he turned his mind resolutely to practical considerations.

The first thing must be to write the official letter. *To Deputy Superintendent of Police Naik. Sir, I beg herewith to tender my resignation from Bombay City Police to take effect one month from today's date. My reasons for the aforesaid action are entirely of a private nature. I am, sir, your obedient servant, GV Ghote, Inspector.*

To go straight to the office now. To take a sheet of official notepaper, to roll it into the typewriter, to type those words out, to check them for errors, to add his signature, to leave the letter in the DSP's IN tray. That would be that.

He waited to cross the traffic-jostling street.

He had some leave due, he thought. He must go through his diary to check exactly how much. But he would certainly not have to work the whole of his resignation month. He might in fact be let go in a day or two. If the DSP felt reasonably disposed towards him.

And would he be? Well, he had worked hard on the Squad. He really had. He had never murmured at being asked to work in the evenings, day after day. He had never even requested, like one super-efficient officer, for time off to take his wife to Mahableshwar. But, on the other hand, there had been that appalling business of the "actress" down in Colaba. Had that been forgotten in the last six months?

But, worse than that, had the DSP developed any idea that this subordinate of his had systematically made him the target of suspicions? That he had contemplated him as the betrayer of the Bats' secrets? If he had the least notion of that, from the way he had been looked at, from having detected that his desk drawers had been searched and his wastepaper basket rifled, then he could make life thoroughly unpleasant until the very last day of his service had been reached. And to have to go on with the grind of making himself be suspicious of every person he met, that would be misery indeed.

He contrived to make his way across the road.

And after today, he thought, there is the question of finding work. Mr. Rao was right about that. Jobs were not easy to get. And they would be even harder if he could not bring into use his police experience, his acquired knowledge of the art of distrusting, of sniffing out.

And where would they all live when they had to leave the house? And Ved, where would he find another cricket team to play for when he no longer qualified for Government Quarters No 4 Under-Elevens? And would there be money to spare for such things as cricket fees with no regular pay coming in?

But at least Protima would be away from that man. That would be worth all the misery that undoubtedly lay ahead. To have broken the fellow's hold on her, to have removed—

His mind unreeled from this reverie with snickering speed. Someone was plucking and plucking at his sleeve in the crowd.

He looked sharply round.

The wrinkled, knowing monkey face of Moti Chiplunkar, boss of the boy pickpockets, was peeking up at him.

"Inspector Ghote, Inspector Ghote, take no notice but listen only. I have a thing to tell that would do you much good in your work. Do not look at me, but listen only."

XIII

For a moment Ghote felt tempted to give the squat little pickpocket at his side a cuff and tell him to get out of his sight. He
wanted at this instant nothing else than to be alone with his misery,
to reel out plan after plan in his head, each driving him more se-
curely into the pit that he at once hated and longed for.

To have cast off the police life once and for all: that was what
he wanted. That and nothing else. To be rid of the burden, though
it had once seemed to be no burden but the beginning and end
of everything. To tear off inch by inch that all-covering skin of
suspiciousness and to become an ordinary person again.

What did he want with such a fellow as Moti Chiplunkar? To
have dealings with him would mean having once more to bring
that dreaded cast-of-mind to bear again. It would mean assessing
what a thief and a liar was saying and wriggling through to his
real motive. It would mean finding a counter and disguising it and
then getting past the fellow's own suspicions. It was too great a
burden to bear.

But something held back the cuffing hand. The remnant of his
past, the habit too engrained to be thrown off in an instant.

"What scheme are you plotting now, Moti Chiplunkar?" he
asked with feigned brutality.

And it was enough. He was enmeshed.

"Sahib. Inspectorji. Would I plan a scheme before you? Before
the only man who was just with me? Maharaj, I would sooner
they cut off my right hand."

"It will be more than your right hand that is cut off, lover of
your mother," Ghote replied, pursuing without thought the tone
that might in an exchange of coarse insults enable him to fathom
the pickpocket's real intentions.

"Maharaj, it is for your good. Maharaj, it is a recompense. From me to you, you and no one else, Maharaj."

Then something in the pickpocket's manner, some tiny hint of uncharacteristic behaviour, hit home to Ghote. Why was the fellow anxious? What did those half-concealed darts of apprehension all round mean? Surely, it must be that he was scared. He was scared of being seen talking to a police inspector.

Then had he really something to say after all? Was he, despite everything his previous record indicated, turning informer?

Ghote walked slowly on, doing all that he could to seem to be simply absorbed in his own thoughts. He glanced up at the high front of the Eros Cinema as he got to it and paused, wrinkling his eyes, as if he was concerned only to see what foreign film was showing and who was in it.

The French Connection. That was some gangster affair surely? Something to do with a huge drug-smuggling racket in America? What a world of romance that was.

"Maharaj," said the quiet voice at his elbow. "I am hearing you are on anti-smuggling now. Maharaj, there is a fellow who used to be a friend of mine, until he . . . But no matter. Maharaj, two days ago I took from his pocket a letter. I am going to drop that on the ground."

Ghote quickly began going through a pantomime of trying to remember the film's title and stars, staring up at the cinema front. Then he turned. The squat little pickpocket, weaving with his life-long skill through the moving crowds, was already some yards away. From the arm of his by no means clean red shirt there slid a pellet of paper. Balled hard together, it dropped almost as straight as a pebble.

Ghote, his mind now working at its fastest, dipped his hand into his trouser pocket and pulled out all the loose coins he had. For a moment or two he examined them as he walked slowly onwards, as if he was wondering whether he had enough cash to make some small purchase. Then, when he judged that his steps had brought him to the spot where the little balled-up wad of paper lay, he contrived to sway into the path of someone behind him so that his elbow was jogged. A couple of coins jinked from his open palm to the ground below.

With a sharp curse, he stooped and scrabbled for them. And

he had judged it exactly. Moti Chiplunkar's gift lay only six inches away from one of his two coins. No one could possibly have noticed as he scooped it up.

He read it sitting inside one of the travel agents' shops a little farther along Vir Nariman Road. The counter was conveniently tourist-besieged, and he was able to settle down on one of the black, well-sprung benches in a totally plausible manner.

Sudha Auntie is not well. She asks you to come on Friday at 10 pm. Do not be later. You know she has a flat now above Byron Chambers near Cotton Exchange. Mangesh.

Swiftly Ghote slipped the scrap of much-folded paper into his pocket. And then, sitting tranquilly in the air-conditioned coolness, he gave himself over to hard thought.

Was the gift to be trusted? A gift it was certainly, plainly nothing less under its crude disguise than a smugglers' rendezvous for this evening, Friday. Surely Chiplunkar must have some secret motive, though, for handing to the police such a piece of information? A vendetta against some other criminal? Well, if it was that, there was nothing to be lost. Or could it be that someone particularly wanted the whole Bats team to be engaged this evening? That was something that must be kept in mind.

But might it not be, after all, no more than what Moti Chiplunkar had said it was? A gesture of thanks?

And if it was that . . . If it was, then it was a magnificent opportunity poured into his lap. If, as the style of the note and the time it mentioned seemed to indicate, a really large consignment of gold or some other smuggled goods was waiting to be distributed this very night, then a splendid lead had been given them on a trail that ought to lead to the kingpin of a big black-money syndicate. It was an opportunity similar to the one the Bats had been exploiting on the day he had joined them, though this was at a later stage in the distribution chain. Well, one thing was certain. He would not mess this up as he had messed up the other affair when that "actress" had crossed his path.

But, better, he could use this piece of knowledge as he had hoped to use the knowledge he had gained when he had spotted that tall tout at Apollo Bunder. He had been given again a marker dye and with it he could trace the source of the leak as if he was following a thickening and thinning line of bright orange on a black background. He could tell either Kelkar or Nadkarni what he had learnt, and then see what happened. It would mean in all probability losing the seth at the end of the trail. But that would be a price worth paying to eliminate the traitor within.

Excitement buzzed in his veins like a fever. Until the thought came, cold as a shock of water flung on the hot body, that he was not going to stay in the Bats.

But was he now after all? Was this that heaven-sent event that he had longed for, the inconceivable something that would alter the unalterable? No, he recorded soberly. No, it was not. If he were to abandon his resignation in the heat of locating the traitor in the Bats, he would be condemning himself just as before to a lifetime of suspicion. Indeed, after witnessing the downfall of a person such as Inspector Nadkarni or of that true example, Inspector Kelkar, he would never be able to trust a single one of his colleagues in all the rest of the days he might spend in the force. He would go through life deprived of any base, a mere spreader of the vile yellow infection.

Should he do nothing then? Forget he had ever encountered Moti Chiplunkar, let the scrap of paper in his pocket fall to the ground, a tiny piece of rubbish? No, he would never be able to forgive himself afterwards. With a key to the mystery that had cost him so dearly thrust unexpectedly into his hand he must not refrain from turning it in the lock. No, this would be his legacy to the profession that had meant so much to him: to present the force before he left it with the impaled body of the one who had betrayed them all.

So, instead of going back to the office and typing out the letter of resignation that he had composed, he sought a personal interview with DSP Naik.

To him, bracing himself like a swimmer poised over a river in wild spate, he first announced his firm and unchangeable intention of giving up his career in the police. And then he said that he was quite prepared to work out in full his final month.

"Especially, DSP, as I have just come into possession of information that could lead us straight to a big black-money seth."

He saw the DSP's eyes come to shining life in the round softly moustached face. But a hand held up large as a traffic constable's on his striped wooden stand forbade him to go on.

"Very well, Ghote, resign if you must, though I think you are a fool to give up a job like the police. But not one word to me, not one, about what you have just heard."

He sat still in his big chair, looking sadly across the expanse of his desk.

"Ghote," he went on, "you must know as well as I do that there is something very wrong in the Bats. I will not say why this is. Suffice it to add that I hope and hope every day that I can put my finger on a leak that does not involve any of the officers under my command."

"Yes, DSP," Ghote murmured.

If only that could be, he thought. If only it could turn out that neither Nadkarni nor Kelkar was to blame. Nor even poor goose-like Dayabhai, and not even really Rohit Radwan who was after all a policeman as well as somebody who had some sort of hold over Protima.

What was that? What could it be?

But the DSP was continuing.

"So this is what I want you to do. Tell me nothing. Tell no one anything, until you have to. Then keep a close check on exactly what you say."

His hands on the wooden arms of his chair clutched suddenly tightly.

"And come to me with a name," he said. "Come with one single name and I will do the rest."

He stared fixedly at the ink-spattered green blotter in front of him. Then he looked up with a glare of ferocity.

"Now, get out," he snapped. "Get out and get on with it."

Ghote left, hurrying not so much because of the DSP's sudden gust of fury as out of respect for the feelings that had produced it.

But were those feelings really genuine, he asked himself as he stood outside in the wide corridor. Were they—the suspicions flew out from their dark clustering places—were they all just an act? It might still be that DSP Naik himself was the man who was selling out on them. Say the seth out of Juhu had gone scurrying from his bungalow not because he had received a direct warning but because of some sixth sense that he was in danger. Then the narrowing-down to either Kelkar or Nadkarni would no longer apply. And then the DSP would once again be back in the running. And Dayabhai. And Radwan.

A grimness set in on Ghote's features like soft earth hardening under a pitiless sun. He was bound to his trade for just a little longer and he must endure experiencing all the distrust and suspicions that went with it.

Ghote decided that it would be Inspector Nadkarni to whom he first entrusted his information that a black-money hoard would be found in all likelihood in a flat above an office block called Byron Chambers somewhere near the Cotton Exchange that very evening. He had chosen Nadkarni after anxious inward debate. Which of them, Kelkar or Nadkarni, should he expose first to the test? Which to weigh first in the gift that had been unexpectedly thrust into his hands like a pair of bazaar merchant's scales? But these were scales that he could not allow himself with a cleverly concealed pressure of the little finger to make weigh unfairly. So in the end he had plumped for Nadkarni, simply because by a hairsbreadth he was the one he would least like it to be.

He contrived to catch him just as he was making preparations to leave the office, for once not much after the correct time. Cursing and hating himself for the deceit, he told him about the incident with Moti Chiplunkar and how he had gone to DSP Naik with the information. But he implied that the whole of the Squad was taking part in an operation the DSP had launched.

He ended by saying that, although the DSP had been anxious not to load Nadkarni with more than his current work, he himself would be extremely grateful if he could come with him later in the evening to the Cotton Exchange. He allowed it to be understood that he harboured a fear of making an error similar to that he had made with the Colaba "actress."

"Inspector," old Nadkarni said, "I do not think you are still needing somebody to hold your hand."

"But—"

"No, you sometimes give the impression that you are uncertain. But I am inclined to think it is only a sort of sacrifice to bring you good luck. However, if you want me, certainly I will accompany you."

Ghote felt a prick of remorse sharp as a thorn at this. But he was nevertheless secretly glad that he had succeeded in a task he would once have thought impossible, tricking Inspector Nadkarni.

He had hoped to rush away the moment the deed was done. To stay long afterwards in the company of that patient old extractor of truth would, he felt, be more than he could survive. And besides he wanted to give the creature in the trap ample time to make the move that would betray him. Or he did not want to.

But Nadkarni did not let things take this easy course.

"My dear chap," he said, "nine o'clock should be ample time to be up in the Cotton Exchange area. So since I shall now have to stay out late I shall take the opportunity of going through more of these First Information Reports. After all, your lead may not come to anything, and then we shall need something dug out of one of these."

He tapped the fat pile on his desk and looked up at Ghote.

"Would you care to assist me?" he asked.

There was no alternative. Nothing was said, but it was plain to Ghote that Nadkarni was in fact taking firm precautions not to be seen to have the least chance of leaking the information that had now been passed on to him. He even had to sit there while the old inspector telephoned his home and told his wife, with a terseness that was almost insulting and could not possibly have concealed a message, that he would not be back till a late hour.

Was this not really proof that Nadkarni was not his man, he asked himself as he sat there listening to the call being made and squirming. And at once dark counterthoughts came dancing out. No, this might simply be proof that Nadkarni was taking precautions.

They worked at the reports. They went, on Nadkarni's suggestion, to the canteen and ate a meal together. And in the end he had to take violent steps to create an opportunity for the fatal slip to be made. "One moment, Inspectorji, if you please," he said. "A call of nature."

And he scuttled out, ran helter-skelter down the stairs and hid himself for a full ten minutes in the lavatory.

Well, he reflected as at just before nine o'clock he and Inspector Nadkarni alighted from a bus in Abdul Rahman Street, I did give him a clear chance to make a warning telephone call. And even if I had not, perhaps in a few minutes he would have made one for himself. When we find this Byron Chambers flat no doubt I shall discover whether a warning did go out or not.

But he was not done with doubts and counterdoubts. Nadkarni, he remembered, had been sitting at his desk when he had returned from that ten-minute absence and the pile of First Information Reports waiting to be dealt with had decreased considerably. Of course, nothing could be easier than to transfer a fat batch from the pending pile to the dealt-with pile. But the thought of Inspector Nadkarni permitting himself anything as slipshod was somehow impossible to contemplate. So had his old mentor not taken advantage of the opportunity created for him? Perhaps he had not. Certainly, he would not have dared to telephone anybody from the office. It would be too easy to check with the switchboard whether any calls had been made.

And if he had not made a call, did this mean he was innocent or doubly guilty? Had he been merely creating an impression of guiltlessness? That would be just what a really cunning man would have done. And for cunning you would have to go a long way to beat Nadkarni.

So was he about to take a much less obvious opportunity now to get a warning through? After all, if he was the betrayer, he would have to act quickly. If the Bats got hold of the name of whoever would be distributing the smuggled goods from the Byron Chambers flat, it might be very difficult to stop them getting on to the seth behind him.

Well, at least he was here beside Nadkarni.

In the warm night he moved so near to him that they were almost touching as they walked. They had just entered the narrow and in daytime traffic-crowded Kalba Devi Road and the tall mass of the Cotton Exchange was visible some three or four hundred yards down on their left. It was a matter now of looking at the buildings on either side to locate whatever elderly office block it was that bore the name Byron Chambers. If it was not on Kalba Devi Road itself, they had agreed, it could not be far off. Otherwise that guarded rendezvous note about Sudha Auntie and her illness would have been more specific.

The pavements were, even at this hour, still well crowded. People were spilling off them here and there on to the roadway where there were comparatively few cars. So it was not unnatural to walk as closely as he was to Nadkarni. He was glad it was not. He was by no means sure how the cunning old devil would get a message away. But he would watch him as if he were a suspect from whom he was intent on getting an unspoken admission of guilt, a single twitch of a facial muscle, hands clasped too hard together, a foot not able to be kept from nervously tapping.

Would there be some sort of sentry outside Byron Chambers? A lounger or an urchin of some kind? Would they signal some sort of alarm to whoever was waiting in the top flat? Was there an escape route over the roofs for the heavy load of gold or shaving blades or whatever contraband it was? It was possible.

Ghote's eyes roamed hard over the pavements in front of them. There were people drifting. There were people hurrying on errands, going out to buy things or coming back with things bought, clutching vegetables in crumpled newspaper or balancing carefully a new supply of flour or rice or dahl. There were respectable people, clerks and shopkeepers in white shirts and trousers or white kurta and dhoti and women in saris with the ends taken decorously over their heads. There were less respectable people, the bare-chested coolies, pigeon-toed and ribby, the occasional prostitute, garish with cheap jewellery and heavily painted eyes, and the boys, a few in the same trade as the chuklas, others semiprofessional pickpockets and sneak thieves. Always ready these to earn a few paise by keeping an eye open for anybody who might be a police officer in plain clothes.

Then, as they were passing the heavy spire-crowned bulk of the Mumba Devi Temple, across the roadway Ghote spotted the words BYRON CHAMBERS. Lit by the intermittent flash of a neon sign advertising a pharmacy, they were deeply cut into the stone above the doorway of a building just off the road itself.

Ghote glanced at Inspector Nadkarni without betraying what he had seen.

If he wants to give his warning, he thought, he will have to act almost at once.

They walked on a few steps. The old inspector's eyes were methodically observing the street ahead. Neither of them spoke.

Then Nadkarni tapped him on the forearm.

"There, Inspector," he said. "Across the road. The neon sign shows it up."

"Good," Ghote said. "Good."

But was it good, he asked himself. What did it mean that Nadkarni had apparently pointed out Byron Chambers just as soon as he had seen those incised words? Oh, God, why could things never be simple?

"Well, Inspector," he said to Nadkarni, drearily pushing on with his task. "Will you go and take station somewhere on the far side? Then we would be doubly sure of spotting any courier."

"No, Inspector," Nadkarni answered at once. "I really see no point in us separating. If we retrace our steps a little and place ourselves just in the temple precincts, somewhere near the corner of the tank, then we would be able to see that doorway quite clearly. And at the temple we would not draw attention to ourselves by loitering."

"First-class idea," Ghote said, pumping into his voice a simple enthusiasm that he was far from feeling.

They turned and walked back to the huge temple and stationed themselves, each with an air of quiet and even prayerful contemplation, at a point not far from the near corner of the big tank that lay with its water gleaming and tranquil under the soft night air. Here and there worshippers moved quietly about, some murmuring the repetitive burble of a prayer, some carrying newly bought garlands of marigolds or jasmine to place at a favoured spot or upon a favourite guru. The sound of tinkling bells and a tapped drum floated to them. There was an atmosphere of removed-from-the-world calm. And they had an excellent view of Byron Chambers.

The minutes passed. Across the roadway the entrance to the building was illuminated at regular fifteen-second intervals by the red glow of the nearby neon sign.

Ghote experienced alternately a turbulent cutting despair and periods of modest content. For as long as he was able to keep his mind on the job of watching the entrance to Byron Chambers he felt relaxed and even happy. This was work he knew. Keeping observation. Subjecting any single person who came within a prescribed area to critical scrutiny. He had done it hundreds of times before, and he wished life had been such that he would do it hundreds of times again.

But life had not been like that. And, as that thought came to him every so often, the fury scoured and scoured through his mind. No, life had dealt him this full flush of suspicion and he was here, not to keep observation, but to trick a colleague, the colleague who had taught him the best part of all he knew.

At last it grew near the rendezvous time obliquely given in the letter about the state of Sudha Auntie's health. Ghote felt tension mounting in a series of abrupt jerks within him. This was going to be the moment of proof for Inspector Nadkarni. If no one came to the rendezvous, then it would be clear that a warning had been got through. And certainly no one but Nadkarni could have given such a warning.

Time passed and then, across the tranquil air over the tank, the sound of a clock beating out the ten strokes of the hour came clear and reverberant.

Ghote, standing with head bent reverently still, strained his eyes to that distant doorway, alternately a deep black shadow and a glowing red under the neon's glare.

No one.

No one had come. The warning must have gone out.

"Arvind," he said.

He had never used Nadkarni's forename before. He had never dared to. Yet he was not uttering it now in contempt. Far from it. It was a cry. A cry of farewell.

"Arvindji, it is past ten."

And Nadkarni turned and smiled at him. It was a smile he knew of old. A smile he had been given many a time in his early months with the CID. Nadkarni's gentle pointing out that he had blundered, perhaps more through overwillingness than through incompetence.

"My dear chap, I did not think I still had to teach you how to wait."

"To wait?" Ghote stammered.

"Yes, my dear chap, to wait. What is wrong with you tonight? You have not seemed at all your usual self. It is now two or three minutes past the hour only. Who outside of the police keeps an appointment to the minute?"

Ghote relaxed. It was absurd. Of course, he would have to—

"Arvind. Look."

"Yes. I have seen."

It was a man going into Byron Chambers. A man about whom there was little to remark. Except to trained eyes. To Ghote and to Inspector Nadkarni there was, by unspoken agreement, no doubt: he was a man up to no good.

XIV

Ghote and Nadkarni had known at once from tiny signs they were used to reading, the quick look backwards, the just overhasty seeking of shadow, that the man they had seen going into the intermittently neon-lit entrance of Byron Chambers was a smugglers' courier. He must be, they realised, someone with a solid wad of black money, most probably in a flat cloth pouch round his waist, coming to exchange it for a gold-smuggler's waistcoat or a large suitcase packed perhaps with highly desired foreign-made shaving blades. But this knowledge was confirmed and confirmed again during the course of the next three hours as they kept watch from their position near the glass-smooth tank of the Mumba Devi Temple. At intervals of more or less exactly half an hour—"These fellows are very good timekeepers," Nadkarni commented, "it must be a particularly efficient organisation"—different men came to the building. Each entered, with those characteristic little signs of furtiveness, went up no doubt to the top floor where light showed behind thin green curtains, and shortly afterwards came out again. And then each of them was walking with the peculiar gait of a man going about with a waistcoat wrapped round him that weighed a good twenty-five pounds.

"Yes, gold undoubtedly," Nadkarni had said when the first of them had emerged. "Does the DSP want us to follow the man up in the flat? Or is one of the others on duty for that?"

"No, that is up to us," Ghote had answered.

He had wished with all his heart that he could tell Nadkarni there and then that DSP Naik had no idea where they were and that no one else in the Bats was anywhere near. He had wanted to come out plainly with the fact that the object of this operation was not to follow a trail that should lead to a seth but to unmask the traitor within their own ranks. And he had known there was now no reason to keep this secret any more. Nadkarni had been cleared. But Ghote had found he was no longer capable of making a spontaneous gesture of trust. An instinct, embedded in him now, forbade him to pass on anything he had discovered to anyone other than, in due course, Mr. Rao.

And that information—it was then that he had seen it, with a coldness that had seemed suddenly actually to lower his body temperature—was that the man who had sold police secrets time and again to different black-money seths was Inspector Kelkar. It was Kelkar, his example for always of what the truly effective police officer should be.

But he had said nothing of that to old Nadkarni. He had told his lie out and between them they had kept watch on the flat above Byron Chambers for all the rest of the night.

Yet at the earliest possible moment in the morning he had made an excuse and gone back to the office. Kelkar was always in his seat before anyone else and he wanted to see him.

He had decided in the long hours of watching that he must give himself absolute proof that his elimination process had no flaw in it. He would subject Kelkar to the same test as he had subjected Nadkarni. Then, when it had trapped him, as surely it must, then he would know beyond the least doubt. Then he would go to Mr. Rao and set in motion the machinery that before long would bring Inspector Kelkar, spruce, neat, driving like a frigate, to the cells on a charge of corruption.

He found, when he had to do it, that he could lie to Kelkar as effectively as he had lied to patient old Nadkarni. And he used much the same tale, suitably updated. He told him that he had had a lucky break and had been able to locate an agent in possession of a considerable sum of black money at this moment in a flat above a set of offices near the Cotton Exchange.

And he contrived—how he had had the daring to sail in under Kelkar's guns in this fashion he never knew—to pour out this information without saying at all where the flat was exactly. Again he implied that DSP Naik had organised full-scale surveillance. And finally he asked Kelkar if he would give him his personal assistance in tracking the agent when he left.

In a moment they were going down the stairs as fast as their legs would take them. And within five minutes at the outside they were in Kelkar's car and heading for the Cotton Exchange.

Ghote sat in silence as they moved through the morning traffic, getting along faster than any other vehicle near them even though only once did Kelkar overtake on the wrong side. He felt oppressed by the very nearness of the man. Something seemed to radiate from him, an extra vitality that ought not ever to be shattered. It might in fact be no more than the fresh tang of his shaving cream or even of the toothpaste that earlier had made his teeth gleam so decisively. It might be no more than the brisk odour of the polish on his immaculately shining shoes. But whatever it was it brought home to Ghote the terribleness of the betrayal that he was engineering.

Because even if the man was guilty, Ghote thought miserably, he had already done so much for the CID. He had raised the morale of the whole department as if he were a super-edition of the acrobats' strong man, lifting on a broad clean back with arm muscles smoothly bulging a weight ten times his own. To trap such a man would be to cast a black shadow on all the work they all were doing. It would be a setback for the whole notion of pursuing wrongdoers without rest till they got their just deserts, of fighting the evil and the twisted and gaining victories.

Could it be possible that it was not Kelkar?

They cut in ahead of a taxi being furiously driven by grinning Sikh. They were not so close in front as to risk a collision, but they were near enough to gain every foot of advantage from the dash of the manoeuvre.

"Just where exactly is the DSP now?" Kelkar asked abruptly.

Ghote's mind seemed to dry up to pea-size. Had Kelkar spotted something wrong in his story of this fake operation? If anyone could, it would be him. He would thrust to the heart of the puffy falsehood.

"The DSP?" he heard himself ask, and heard himself sound foolish asking.

"Yes, man. Is it that he has decided not to come out on the operation?"

Ghote thought like a spinning wheel. To say that the DSP was out in the field somewhere? Or to say that he had decided not to come? Surely it was more likely that he would be out, if the Bats really were about to bring off their major success at last?

He had opened his mouth to begin the lie when some last-instant caution made him change his mind.

"Ye— No," he said. "No, the DSP appeared to think it would be sufficient for him to exercise general supervision only."

They had been caught at some lights, which at that moment changed to green. Kelkar shot away from them as if he was at the start of a high-speed chase.

"I cannot understand that man," he said.

"DSP Naik?" Ghote asked, genuinely shocked at his companion's tone of brisk dismissal.

"Who else, Inspector? You know, all these last weeks he has stayed stuck in his seat. What is wrong with the fellow?"

"Perhaps after that Pujari business he is being careful only," Ghote suggested.

"Of course he is, man. But being careful is not going to get anyone anywhere. Sitting on his bottom all day."

"No," Ghote concurred demurely.

He could not help applying it all to the man sitting beside him, his eyes pugnaciously assessing the traffic. Had the aggressiveness he showed in every turn of his talk been his undoing? To push forwards and dig out what was wrong was magnificent. But it could lead you into trouble. Indeed, the DSP had found that precisely over the Baddu Pujari business. And to a large extent through Kelkar's quickness to pounce too. So he had drawn in his horns. Really, it was sensible. But had Kelkar at some time failed to do just that? Had he pushed too far somewhere and become enmeshed in something too sticky and clinging even for him to force his way out of? It had happened to other good officers. They had gone past the limit and laid themselves open to blackmail by criminal elements.

Could it be that Kelkar was being blackmailed into providing information to the criminal community from the heart of the Black-money and Allied Transactions Squad itself? Well, perhaps quite soon the answer to that question would be made plain.

The car came to a snapping halt beside the kerb exactly in front of the Mumba Devi Temple, where Ghote had said that Inspector Nadkarni was on observation duty.

"You hop out and locate Nadkarni," Kelkar said. "I will find somewhere to put the vehicle so that I can make a quick getaway if we need."

Well, Ghote reflected as he watched Kelkar's Ambassador pull smoothly away into the traffic stream, at least he does not yet know who he would have to warn this time. Only when I tell him the name of the office building will he be in a position to make that telephone call. And then I shall be watching him, every move.

He found Nadkarni, not at the temple but outside the Cotton Exchange. He had made no obvious alteration in his appearance but had unobtrusively become just another elderly babu waiting perhaps for a friend before going in to his clerk's table.

"Ah, you are back again," he greeted Ghote quietly. "Well, so far no one has arrived for any of the offices in Byron Chambers. And our man, whoever he is, has certainly not come out."

"You do not think he has got out some other way?" Ghote asked.

"No, I think you need not trouble yourself in that direction. I have been having a thorough look at the building. That is why you found me along here. And I do not believe there is any way out except by that doorway."

Ghote looked across. The doorway appeared very drab in the morning light. The pharmacy neon, though still winking regularly, no longer lit it.

He told Nadkarni that Inspector Kelkar had arrived to take over with himself.

"Well, goodbye then, my dear fellow," Nadkarni said. "I shall go home and get a little sleep. Try to see that you get a chance to do the same later. You would be tired."

"Yes. Yes. Thank you."

Ghote stood for a moment relishing the almost fatherly advice Nadkarni had given him, and happy to be able to think that now it need not be put to that turning-inside-out scrutiny which he had felt obliged to apply until the night before to every word the old inspector spoke.

He went quickly back to the temple where Kelkar joined him almost immediately. As soon as he arrived Ghote told him the name of the building they were to watch.

Now the test had begun. Now he himself must be tinglingly

alert, not for anyone who might come out of Byron Chambers, but for anything that his fellow watcher might do to send out some sort of a message.

Before long office workers began to enter the drab doorway with the incised words in the stone above it. Ghote, beginning indeed to feel weary after his night without sleep, found it all he could do to pretend an interest in them and at the same time to keep Kelkar under unremitting observation. But they did not have long to wait before the situation changed.

They had been concerned to note accurately the appearance of everybody who went into Byron Chambers so that, when anyone came out, they could be sure who it was. But when their prospective quarry did emerge there could have been no possible doubt about him. He was dressed in the white cassock, black hat and broad black waistband of a Christian priest.

"Well," Ghote said, relieved, "he would not be hard to follow."

"Do not be so sure, Inspector," Kelkar answered. "A fellow like that, with the daring to disguise himself in such a way, I believe I know what sort of a chap he would be. And, listen to me, if once he suspects we are behind him he will lead us a devil of a chase."

Already they were hurrying forward, Ghote keeping close to Kelkar's elbow. They got across the traffic swirl of Kalba Devi Street, its narrowness enabling them, at the cost of scrapingly avoiding going under two different sets of wheels, to nip over without delay. A spate of illegal horning from car, van, and lorry died away behind them. In half a minute they were within twenty yards of the billowy cassocked so-called priest and there was nothing to prevent them closing on him should it be necessary.

Ghote decided to leave the conduct of the chase entirely to Kelkar. So far he had seemed all eagerness. But no doubt he would be planning at some stage to lose their man. Once he had done that, nothing would be more natural than to head for a telephone. And then he could easily get in touch with his underworld contact and make sure, for a price, that the Byron Chambers flat left no trail to the seth.

If that happened, Ghote resolved, it would not be many minutes before he was sending his signal to Mr. Rao and asking for another interview after all.

"Quick."

Kelkar shot out the syllable almost before Ghote had seen what the white-cassocked figure ahead had done to justify it. But it was an emergency all right. The fellow had halted beside a cluster of motor scooters piled up against some railings and was looking over them as if to pick out his own in all the heap of entangled handle-bars, little black-tyred wheels and bouncy steering forks. If he got hold of it quickly he could well be away before Kelkar could return to the car.

But Kelkar was already getting back across the street, striding fearlessly into the pushing, heedless, fumy traffic.

He would have the car ready to take up the chase in time if any-one could. Or would he?

Had he already made the opportunity to get off a warning mes-sage? What to do about it? Keep an eye on the bogus priest, run-ning behind if necessary till the car came up? Or abandon the fellow and track Kelkar?

There could only be one answer: sink the true policeman's instincts.

Ghote swung round and plunged in his turn into the roadway where the traffic had momentarily halted. He cut across in front of a bright red Fiat as it began to move again, slid through a layered obstacle of some dozen or fifteen still-blocked cyclists and dived for the far kerb.

The squeal of sharp brakes rang terribly in his ears. From the far side of a barely moving lorry belonging to the Bombay Cow Cemetery another Fiat had come nipping along on the inside lane. The corner of its hot front bumped heavily into his right thigh as it tried to halt. He staggered and all but fell under its wheels. But twisting desperately he managed to keep on his feet and hurl himself to the far pavement.

Behind him he heard a stream of curses. He paid no attention but, pushing himself upright, turned in the direction he had seen Kelkar take.

Kelkar. He must hold onto the thought of Kelkar. Was he even at this instant slipping into a shop to telephone? Muzzily he shook his head. He felt a strong desire to be sick. His battered thigh seemed mercifully numbed.

Where was Kelkar? Ah, there. And he was getting into his Ambassador, parked just off the main road.

What did this mean? Was it proof he was no traitor? Oh, no. No, he might well have reckoned that it would be cleverer not to lose their man this easily.

Their man. Rubbery-legged, Ghote turned back once again. He almost missed seeing that the traffic beside him had once more come to a complete halt. But, while it was still stationary, impatiently fuming, he forced himself to step once more on to the roadway.

Every engine seemed to be racing just for the purpose of leaping forward and mercilessly flattening him. He fought back against the tide of sickness rising up again inside him. And at last he set foot on the pavement once again.

The mock priest was still attempting to get his own motor scooter free. Left chained to the railings all night it had been at the very centre of the heap. But he was dealing with the chain's padlock now.

Still, Kelkar was coming. Turning, Ghote saw the familiar Ambassador making its way forward with the once-again moving traffic.

Their quarry finally extricated his machine. He bounced it down the kerb into the roadway, hitched his billowing white cassock, swung himself astride the saddle and with a soft roar from the miniature engine slid into the jostling traffic stream. Kelkar brought the Ambassador to a momentary halt, leaning across as he did so and flinging the nearside door open. Ghote scrambled in, sending a jolt of pain up from his bruised thigh, and before he had time to pull the door closed they were off again.

"We are going to have one hell of a job keeping up with that scooter," Kelkar said. "One small gap in the traffic and the fellow could be quarter of a mile ahead while we are still stuck behind some damned lorry."

Ghote reflected that this was certainly true. But, he asked himself at once, could it not be also Kelkar laying down the basis of an excuse for letting their man escape?

They had turned into Abdul Rahman Street and were heading north. The mock priest was not getting particularly fast through the traffic, though fast enough for his white robe to billow out behind him in the wind of his motion. The road conditions Kelkar had spoken of could easily occur at any instant.

"I am going to try to get up and sit on his tail," Kelkar muttered. "If he guesses what we are, so much the worse."

With an adroitness that brought Ghote to a state of wide-eyed admiration, even despite the confusion in his mind, Kelkar cut round on the wrong side of two vehicles in succession and with a savage burst of acceleration emerged within five yards of the white-robed figure perched on the little scooter.

At Bhendi Bazaar their quarry turned left into Sardar Patel Road and their speed of travel increased. But Kelkar never failed to keep the Ambassador within ten yards of the broad back with the soft white cassock bulging out from it.

Ghote felt able to think coherently once again, though his shock and his state of sleeplessness both hovered on the edge of his mind. If I had to lose that scooter, he said to himself, how would I set about it. I would certainly have to appear to be pursuing as hard as I could. Well, Kelkar is doing that. But then what? Seek out some slow-moving vehicle, a big truck or a bus, and deliberately get tucked in behind it? No, much too obvious. Yard by yard, inch by inch almost, to lose ground? Yes, that would be the way.

And at just that moment Kelkar, seeing a momentary gap between the sharp black-and-yellow of a taxi and the looming red of a bus, trod sharply on the accelerator and shot through. The manoeuvre put him within two feet of the scooter.

Was this the action of a man plotting to lose their quarry? Surely not. Or was it? Would they not attract his attention right up behind him like this? And then, as Kelkar himself had said, if he once forced the pace in traffic as thick as this he would be bound to get away. Oh, why for every white must there at once appear an opposite blotting-out black?

But the white-robed man sat looking steadily ahead, picking his way through the traffic at a rate that was decent but no more. Considering what an immense sum in black money he must have underneath that billowing garment, he was being sensible to risk nothing. And that would make it difficult for Kelkar deliberately to lose him.

Ghote sat, letting the turmoil in his mind gradually fade away, nursing his bruised thigh, which did not seem to be as bad as he had at first feared, and waiting for the move to come.

They forked right into the straight run of Falkland Road going up towards Tardeo. The Ambassador was now lying a few yards back from the scooter. But the little machine was still easily within pouncing distance. On they went past the thick-packed houses, over the railway, and on again to Tardeo itself and the looming mass of the Central Station.

"Well," Ghote said, breaking the long silence, "which way will he take here?"

He had not intended to speak. Whatever was said between them would be only one more strand in the bond that tied him to Kelkar, the thick-twined bond of respect, admiration, almost worship. And at any moment now he might have to sever that rope with a single stroke from a thrice-sharpened knife. Yet he had felt an impulsive desire to communicate. He had wanted to affirm that a man as splendid in the police way-of-life, a man who to put it no higher had in the pursuit they were now making forced his way through to hold onto their quarry in the way Kelkar had, could not be the sort of traitor that it seemed that he must be.

"Which way?" Kelkar replied between his teeth, looking at the four possible roads that led from the roundabout they were approaching. "Any way, Inspector. But, be sure, whichever one it is I will hang on to him."

And he did too, following not much more than fifteen yards behind as the white-robed man on the scooter took the road leading roughly north in the direction of the Arabian Sea and the two mighty edifices on the shore, the big-domed Hindu Mahalaxmi Temple and, on its causeway-approached island, the Muslim Haji Ali Mosque.

Soon enough they had come within sight of the sea. They were lying now almost thirty yards back from their quarry. But, taking into account the lesser density of the traffic, they were still within easy reach of him.

Yet, Ghote asked himself, comparing this gap with the few feet only that had separated them when they were down in Sardar Patel Road, was Kelkar even at this moment getting ready for that one apparently accidental manoeuvre that could so easily put their man out of range once and for all. Just let him try.

They were opposite now the triple arched front of the Maha-laxmi Temple. Left or right? Up north along the coast by Hornby Vellard? Or back south into the luxury of Cumballa Hill with at least three good roads to choose from, Warden Road looking out over the sea, or rich Pedder Road, or, lying farther back from the steep plunge to the shore and forking off Pedder Road, Carmichael Road? The latter choice most probably. In one of the splendid flats of Cumballa Hill a man such as the seth who ought to lie at the end of this trail would very likely live.

Yes, the left turn. But was Kelkar really a little too far behind now? The junction of Pedder Road and Warden Road lay ahead. Would they be absolutely sure, as far back as this, of seeing which their man took? Probably. Almost certainly. But not absolutely certainly.

Abruptly Kelkar broke the silence, which had seemed to Ghote to lie like a tension-charged cloud of electricity between them.

"You seem unhappy, Inspector. Not to worry. I can be within a yard of that fellow any time I want."

He seemed utterly confident. Was he? Confident of keeping in sight of that white figure crouching over the small scooter? Or confident of being able to lose him in a manner that looked entirely likely? What he had said had been true enough, certainly. The Ambassador had acceleration enough to roar up to the scooter at any time Kelkar wanted, even from as far back as the hundred and fifty yards that now separated them.

And at that moment, when the scooter was just approaching the fork of Warden Road and Pedder Road and was still neatly in sight, a big furniture removals van which had been coming towards them on the other side suddenly, for no good reason that Ghote could see, swung out of its path and careered across the road straight in front of them.

He caught one glimpse of the driver's face. It was scared silly.

Had he himself been at the wheel of the Ambassador, he recorded afterwards, both he and Kelkar would almost certainly have been killed. His reactions would just not have been fast enough. They would have been into the side of the high furniture van head-on.

But Kelkar's reactions were fast, phenomenally fast. He wrenched at the wheel. And, instead of slamming his foot on the brake, he plunged it on to the accelerator. They shot forward. Their front wing grazed the rearmost corner of the van. The impact bounded them off as if they had been a football slammed hard against a solid goal post. The Ambassador skidded through a half circle and then zoomed back along the road in the direction they had been coming.

Kelkar brought it to a halt within fifty yards. Flinging himself round to look back, Ghote saw the furniture van tipped forward at the side of the road. But of course there was no sign of the white-robed man on the scooter.

Then, to his astonishment, he felt the car moving. Kelkar was swinging it hard round. In seconds they were heading back in the direction of the fork, their speed increasing with every yard.

"We'll try Pedder," Kelkar said.

And he chose right. They had just one glimpse of the billowy-backed white figure before the little scooter had whizzed him round a turning to the right. But they had caught up enough by the time they too reached the corner to be able to see that their quarry had arrived at his destination.

"Fine," said Kelkar simply, as he brought the Ambassador to a discreet halt.

And, fine, fine, fine, echoed Ghote. Fine because the most foolproof opportunity had been offered Kelkar to lose the man they had been following and he had moved heaven and earth not to take it. Fine because Kelkar, the great example, was not guilty of that worst of all betrayals.

Only, if he was not, and Nadkarni was not, who then was?

XV

For some hours after they had tracked down the disguised priest with the wads of black money hidden under his billowy white robe Ghote seriously doubted whether, despite all the evidence, there was a betrayer in the Bats at all.

He had just proved, he told himself, that Inspector Kelkar was as loyal as he was forceful. He had equally given Inspector Nadkarni more than one chance to slip out a warning message to the seth whose flat they had at last located, and Nadkarni had taken none of them. And the affair at Juhu had seemed to show that of all the Bats only Kelkar and Nadkarni could have betrayed them then.

So was it possible that each of the failures the Bats had experienced had been due simply to chance? To believe that would mean accepting an extraordinary series of coincidences. But chance was chance, and there was nothing in strict logic to say that any of the failures could not have been simply pure luck for the seths who had got away.

The prospect of believing that this picked group of policemen was totally guiltless of any betrayal was wonderfully sweet. It would not make him change his mind about resigning because resigning was what was going to get Protima away from that man Radwan. But it made him more content than he had thought he would be again.

It was a feeling that lasted little more than an hour.

During most of that time he had kept a lone watch over the entrance to the flats to which they had traced the black-money courier. He had stood in the hallway, light, bright, clean and airy with an enormous bowl of flowers on a stand against one wall, and he had talked to the gorgeously turbaned chaprassi who was on duty there. They had talked about sexual prowess, Ghote having as the result of one or two cunning questions let it be known that he was the sole vendor of a love-potion of extraordinary strength. Inspector Kelkar in the meanwhile, having been put in the picture over DSP Naik's lack of knowledge about details of this affair, had been hard at work summoning the other Bats for a combined swoop.

It had taken him only a few minutes over the hour. At the end of that time everybody had been in position. Dayabhai Patel, craning forward with excitement, and Rohit Radwan had approached by the servants' staircase which ran up from the back of the entrance hall and the other three of them had gone up in the smoothly humming lift.

"Well, Ghote," Kelkar had said as they emerged on to the marble-floored landing outside the seth's flat, "this is your show, you carry on."

"Thank you."

Ghote had put his thumb fairly and squarely on the stainless-steel bellpush and had kept it there. There had been no answer but he had not necessarily expected one.

"The pair of them will be creeping down into the arms of Radwan and Patel," old Nadkarni had said happily.

"Or they will be hiding somewhere inside," Kelkar had suggested.

"I will give one more ring," Ghote had contributed.

It had been loud and long. Then Kelkar had stepped forward with the short crowbar he had brought with him. The wood at the edge of the door, grained teak though it was, had at once begun to crack with a series of satisfyingly sharp reports.

"This is the police," Ghote had called, making his voice as deeply foghorn like as he could.

But there had come no reaction from the far side of the door. And it was then that the first tiny blossom of doubt flicked into Ghote's mind.

In the next few seconds it grew like a flower opening to the morning sun. There came no sound at all from inside the flat. Kelkar finished bursting the teak door open. He ran in with Ghote at his heels and Nadkarni waiting in the hall as a long stop. The two of them conducted a fierce sacking search of the whole lush apartment, tearing, tugging, and upsetting. But they knew it was going to be no good.

Once again a seth seemingly secure in the claws of the forces of the law had received a warning and got clear away. In the aftermath it had been easy to see how this had happened. Inspector Kelkar had decided, very reasonably, that time was important. It had been easily possible that the seth, once he had received the black money from the man disguised as the priest, would have taken it away almost immediately to some other hiding place. And, although he had no reason to suspect he would be followed, it would not have been easy for Ghote on his own to be certain of keeping him under unseen observation. So the sooner Kelkar had got the whole Bats team there surrounding the flats block the better.

In the circumstances then Kelkar had taken no particular precautions over security. He had simply told the DSP and Dayabhai Patel, who had been in the office when he had got back, and had telephoned to wake Inspector Nadkarni from his well-earned sleep and recall Inspector Radwan from an off-duty spell. And in the subsequent bustle, as Ghote soon found out with a few casual-seeming questions, there had been ample opportunity for each of them to have got in touch with an underworld contact. The DSP himself could easily have done it, even from his own office, as he had elected not to come out on the operation. Both Nadkarni and Radwan could have telephoned from their homes before going to the flats. Dayabhai Patel equally had had several clear opportunities when he had been left on his own.

In short, with the probable exceptions of Kelkar and Nadkarni who had after all rejected chances of sending an earlier warning, all the Bats were once more subjects of legitimate suspicion. Things were simply as bad as they ever had been.

Although by the time the consequences of the seth's escape had been fully dealt with Ghote was feeling very much in need of some sleep, it was without any sort of eagerness that about midday he made his way back home. There was now no matchstick flare of hope even in the darkness that seemed to spread over all his life.

And at home, the home which in a month at the most would

with his resignation no longer be his, he proceeded promptly, with the perverseness of deep fatigue, to make matters even worse.

Protima met him at the door. And at once went as wrong as she could, to his mind, in trying to show him sympathy.

"Ah, it is you at last," she said. "Are you very tired altogether? How did the business go? Rohit was at home when they called him out to take part and he told me that it was your bandobast."

Radwan, he thought. There again. At the heart of his affairs. Radwan, contriving no doubt even as he told her that the swoop on the seth was of his arranging, to hint that it was bound to go wrong. And it had gone wrong.

So, instead of answering what had after all been a tender inquiry, he snapped out.

"What for was Radwan here? What for was the fellow coming talking about office affairs? He has no sense of security whatever."

"But sense of security he has and has," Protima flared back. "He was not telling one single thing of where you were or what you were doing. Only that it was something big and that you were the one who had found it."

But praise was not going to make him happy. Not now that his greyly unrefreshed mind, already marched over by dark sweeping monsters enough, had had sudden sight of the shape of its worst fear of all.

"But what for was that man here?" he demanded, brushing aside everything else Protima had said. "What for, I am asking."

"What for? Because I had called. I had called him to come."

She stood there, straight-backed, proud of mouth, eyes under the fine arches of the eyebrows sparking defiance.

Ghote nearly knuckled under. What was the good of anything? Very nearly he stayed silent and let that disdainful stare mean what it might. But some last glimmer of fire amid his smouldering blazed up.

"You were calling that man into this house?" he said with hammer-stroke loudness. "You are to tell me what for."

He had laid down the challenge. Immediately he wished it could be called back. This was not the moment that he could endure hearing the blackest tidings. Later, another time, when he was less tired, less depressed already, then perhaps he could bear it.

Yet had time rolled back those few seconds and given him an-

other chance, he knew that he would not have said other than
he had. If there was a worst to know, then truly he wanted to have
it there clearly before him.

But Protima by way of answer gave him only a little side-of-
the-mouth smile, flicking like a whip.

"I am asking Rohit about the bats," she said. "Last night they
were altogether terrible. I am telling, one of them came as close
to my head as this."

Ghote stood, almost stupidly, looking at the fine-boned, back-
curving hand as Protima held it within two inches of her sleekly
combed head. And he saw then that into her hair she had twisted
a little spray of jasmine. The almost white flowers were like a tiny
cluster of cool stars against the deep black richness of the thickly
wound hair.

Who they for, those flowers?

"Bats," he spat out. "What is all this talk of bats?"

"I am telling. It was because of the bats that I was asking Rohit
to come in. So many times have I begged and beseeched you to
act against those bats. And always you are doing nothing. And
little Ved dreams of the creatures and wakes screaming in the
night. And then when one of them does what I had told and told
that they would, and comes as near my head as this . . ."

This time the long thin-fingered hand was less than an inch away
from the glossy hair. And from the small cluster of yellowy white
flowers.

"Yes," Ghote shouted. "And who brought the bats here in the
first place? No one but your Rohit. For years those bats had been
content where they were. They were doing no one any harm. And
then that man comes along and stirs them up and makes trouble.
Such trouble of all kinds he makes that I do not care to think
of it even."

"What trouble? What trouble is that?" Protima demanded then,
all drawn up like a lancer at the moment of the charge.

And this time Ghote quailed at the challenge. He fell back instead on the bats again.

"If he had left those bats, that he should have left untouched
as a Muslim, then I am saying and saying there would have been
no troubles."

"But he did not leave them. He is not the man to leave things that he does not like. He chased every bat away from his house. And, now that I have asked, he is going to chase them away from here."

"He is going . . . ?"

Ghote stared at her.

She preened herself, feeding on her success in having touched him so smartingly.

"Yes," she said. "I have asked Rohit if he would deal with those bats since my husband will not. And he at once agreed."

"But it is ridiculous."

"What for ridiculous? Is it ridiculous when those disgusting creatures come and fix their claws in my head?"

"It is ridiculous," Ghote explained more coolly, thinking of the considerable difficulties in even getting near the bats, "because in four weeks only we are leaving this house."

"And for four whole weeks you are happy to leave me to be tormented? Other husbands would not leave for four hours. Rohit will come tonight when he is off duty."

"He will not."

"He will. I have asked. He has said. He will come."

"He will not."

"And I say that he will."

Again she stared him in the face. He felt she was daring him to put the real question the situation demanded "Why is Rohit Radwan coming to do this for you especially?" Answer: "Because he is my lover."

He stood and faced her, with the familiar items of his household life in their familiar places in the room behind her, all too soon to be brutally displaced. He saw the cane-edged table and the slip of tile that always was jammed under the far leg to stop it rocking. He saw on it in their time-hallowed places the old grunting fan in its wire cage and the radio with its dial pointer at the angle for that wretched Vividh Bharati programme that Ved would listen to whenever he got the chance. "Inspector Eagle" indeed and his ridiculous adventures. His gaze took in the two cupboards, every scratch and patch in their paintwork absolutely familiar, a constant nag and yet in a way loved. He saw the green curtain that hung in the doorway to their bedroom, its pattern one of their successes as joint purchasers on a shopping expedition long, long ago now. He took in even the very window bars, rusted and painted over and rust-stained over the paint. He saw them all and he felt with every tiny cube of his flesh how much stood at this moment in jeopardy.

No, he could not go to the final length. He could not ask for the answer "Because he is my lover."

He went past her into the room and his hands went to the buttons of his shirt. He began to undo them one by one with a tremendous heavy calmness.

"What is that you are doing?" Protima demanded.

"I am getting out of my good clothes."

Protima slipped from her attitude of armour-sparkling defiance.

"Well, yes," she said, with a little uncertainty. "You are tired. You would want to sleep. But do not undress here. Go to bed."

"I am not going to bed. I am not undressing so as to sleep. I am changing my clothes, not taking them off."

"Changing them? But what for?"

"Because if I am going to climb the neem tree by the godown and scramble along that old and filthy wall to deal with those bats, it is no sense wearing my best shirt and trousers."

"But no. No there is no need. Rohit will climb up there. You sleep. You are tired."

"I am not tired," Ghote shouted in a voice that rang round and round the little room.

He felt the iron bands of fatigue grow tighter round his forehead even as his voice still resounded in the confined space.

What if I fall climbing up there: the thought ballooned up in his head. High up there I will need to have all my reflexes at their keenest. I will fall. Tired as I am, I am bound to fall.

What do I care if I do? What have I got to go on living for? My career, my only chosen way of life, is finished. And what has that way of life become in any case? Traitors eat at its heart. The Bats, the choicest team ever picked from all the police of Bombay, harbours within it a man who has sold its secrets. Sold them. And when I was given the task of finding him out, finding him out from among five, I failed. I got nowhere. Yes, let me die.

But no. No, I have got something to go on living for. I have Ved. And more I have Protima. I have her. I know I have. All that lover talk is not true. I know it is not. I know it is not.

Yet I am going to go up that tree. I am going to get across the gap to the wall of the godown. I am going to risk hanging from those eaves all covered in slimy bats' droppings. I am going to rout out those creatures before— Before anyone else.

He said nothing more to Protima but went into the bedroom. In the almira there, just where in the back of his mind he remembered that Protima kept such things, he found an old shirt and his oldest pair of trousers. He put them on, recollecting sourly as he did so that he had not indeed worn the trousers since that fateful Ganpati Day when Mr. Rao had accosted him on antipickpocketing duty. That seemed an era ago now. It had been a different era too. Things had been simpler. Police work had meant just catching criminals, bringing such powers as he had and what techniques he had learnt to the task and no more. The torture of suspecting his own colleagues, of distrusting everything they did and said had been something then that he could not have conceived of. Doubting Nadkarni and Kelkar, those twin pillars. Cancelling his friendship with poor Dayabhai. Regarding Rohit Radwan he knew not how. Even looking at DSP Naik with a yellow-tinged eye. How far he had travelled, and on what a road.

As soon as he had done up the last button he marched out to the back of the house. He noticed Protima in the kitchen, standing by the tap. He even saw the one stifled gesture of protestation that she made. But not by the least movement of a muscle did he betray that he had been in any way affected.

He clambered over the sagging wire of the boundary fence and went and inspected the task before him. Strictly, the gap between the neem tree and the godown wall was not absolutely too wide to get across. If it had been a matter of jumping the distance from the firm ground on which he now stood, he would not have worried. But up there it would be a question of taking off from some thin, rocking, slippery branch and of catching hold of some projection on the old dark stone wall. How long had the godown been there? Its stone was almost black, cut in great slabs. And the ancient mortar between them had hardened till it was as unyielding. The place must have been built as long ago as the great expansion of Bombay in the days of the American Civil War when suddenly Manchester and all England had cried out for cotton and the city had shot up like a grove of young bamboos.

And there at the top of the blank smooth surface were the bats. They were hard to see in the sunlight, hard to pick out as individual beasts. But the bulk of them, irregular, black, shifting at times a little, occasionally emitting a muffled squeak, was clear enough. And he could detect the smell too, sharp and tangy. What would it be like up among them, with all those yard-wide leathery wings flapping and beating?

But he had to go. And there was no point in hanging about. He pushed his way back through the interlacing growth of grasses and thorny bushes and pulled out of the boundary fence a length of thick bamboo. Then he made his way over to the neem and began to heave himself up into it.

In a very short time he was high in the tree's heart. From this vantage, with the cool odour of the dark and glossy leaves blotting out every trace of the bats' stink, he surveyed his position again. It looked no better.

The gap across to the godown wall was horribly wide. The wall had few projections big enough to grab. The ground below was, he knew, baked iron hard. A broken arm? He forced the vision of the protruding end of splintered bone out of his mind. Concussion? A broken back? The pelvis?

But he must take the risk. Or come tamely to the conclusion that routing out the bats was not practicable. Then he would have to climb down back to the ground, go back into the house, mutter a word of explanation to Protima and go off to bed. But it would not be to sleep. He would not sleep now. And in the evening Radwan would come.

He had no doubt that Radwan would climb up, get across to that wall somehow, send the bats on their way to disgust and terrify someone else and get back again in perfect safety. It would be just the sort of thing the fellow did.

And then? Then would he not go to the house, give one insolent jerk of his head to Protima and lead her across to the house on the other side of the road? That empty, wifeless house.

The vision was too clear in Ghote's mind for him to do anything else but take the branch of the neem that looked thickest and push himself out along it. Let him fall.

XVI

What happened when Ghote had squirmed along the ever-thinning branch of the neem was almost laughable in its simplicity. He had inched and inched forward till the bending branch had eventually placed him with head lower than his feet and his extended body pointing poised at the hard ground below. But his weight, moving constantly outwards, had also pulled down the topmost branches of the tree above him. It had pulled them down and outwards till the thin agitating tips had flicked at the outer edges of the sleeping bat horde on the wall of the godown. First one bat had stirred angrily. Then the next of the downward-hanging, dog-faced creatures had stirred. And before long the infection had spread to the whole deep, dense, hanging mass.

Ghote, his face globuled with sweat, looking along the tapering branch in front of him and wondering how he could go even a foot more along it, let alone stand up and jump, had heard the growing chorus of indignant squeaks above him. He twisted his neck round now and contrived to peer upwards. And when he saw what was happening he realised how he could solve his problem.

He pulled his short bamboo stake from where he had tucked it into his shirt and let it fall. Then he eased himself backwards a foot or two till his perch was more secure and reached out and selected a long thin branch from the tree beside him. It took him nearly ten minutes to twist and tear it off but eventually he had in his hands a long, thin, pliable switch.

And then, swish, swish, whack, whack, in less than half a minute the prick-eared creatures on the godown wall began to shift and to squeak. And then first one left its hanging place, leathery wings extending in the hard glare of the unaccustomed sunlight, and then another. Soon they were leaving by the half dozen and the dozen. And at last in a dense, squeaking, enraged mass they were all off, flying from the accursed spot, going, leaving the place, seeking a new black-shaded refuge, defeated, disgraced, routed utterly.

But at that moment Ghote's slim branch had borne his weight too long. There was a sudden lurch and he found himself almost upside-down, clinging on for dear life with clutching hands and hard-entwined legs. All the way down his back there slithered something more solid than a leaf. It flicked him on the ear as it fell to the ground and, mesmerised, he watched it tumble. It was a wallet.

He had just realised that it must be, of all things, the wallet that he had saved from Moti Chiplunkar's thieving fingers that long ago Ganpati Day and had shoved into his back pocket and since utterly forgotten when, with a thin high creak of living wood torn from living wood, his branch finally parted from the neem's trunk. But the parting was slow, wonderfully slow. And his downward plunge was thus slow too. It was slow enough for the thin branches farther down to delay his fall, slow enough for him to grab in passing at any slender twigs that came within reach. And, though each time he felt the leaves on them rip away under his clutch, they enabled him somehow to twist over in the air. So when he reached the ground it was not head foremost but more or less right way up.

He hurt himself. He twisted his left ankle till the pain jabbed atrociously. But he broke nothing and only collected a fresh crop of bruises, mostly on his seat, to add to the long purple patch on his thigh where the Fiat had hit him crossing Kalba Devi Street.

He sat where he had landed, feeling sick. In a minute or so he heard Protima calling. He turned his head carefully. She was getting over the wire fence, having considerable difficulty with her sari.

"Are you all right, Husbandji?" she shouted. "What have you broken?"

Ghote looked over at her, feeling despite the shock and the sickness in his stomach, a great welling of tenderness.

"Yes, I am quite all right," he said. "No harm done, you know. And the bats have gone."

"Yes, yes. I saw. I saw. I was watching from the window of the kitchen. You did wonderfully. Wonderfully."

Then Ghote, who knew that to look out from the tiny window

of the kitchen it was necessary to hoist oneself up on to the gas cylinder in the corner and then to twist round at a painfully cramped angle, saw that he had not lost by even the tiniest amount the trust, sympathy, and love of his wife. The jasmine stars in her hair were for him and had been put there for no other.

When she came up he continued to sit where he was and smiled at her like a baby.

"Listen," he said, to dispel the last of the anxiety in her eyes, "when I fell a little wallet slipped out of my back pocket and came down first. It is just over there. Could you fetch it?"

Protima picked her way through the scratchy grass and thorns and retrieved the small, glossy, black-leather object. Ghote took it from between her fine fingers and examined it.

"Look," he said, "it is not truly a wallet after all . . . It is a notebook. A notebook full of figures, pages and pages of them. I wonder is the owner's name in it."

But, though before getting eventually to his feet he flipped through every page of the chubby little leatherbound book, he found no indication of who the woman he remembered dropping it could be.

With Protima's solicitous aid, he limped back towards the house and at last his bed. In the distance a few of the bats could still be seen wheeling angrily in the unaccustomed daylight. They looked as if they were making for their old haunt in the trees behind Inspector Radwan's house.

Just before he dropped off to sleep in the darkened bedroom Ghote gave a deep chuckle, tinged a little with malice.

It was the next morning before Ghote finally surfaced from his deep sleep. He woke feeling stiff and a little sore in hips and twisted ankle. But he was filled with a song of triumph which, tell it to behave and be quiet though he might, would not be stilled.

Ridiculous, he thought, to feel like this about a victory over nothing more than a bunch of stinking squeaky bats. But feel like it he did and nothing could quell the feeling.

From beside him Protima got up, seeming to find at once as always her accustomed easy litheness. Through eyes still half closed he could see beyond her the alarm clock on its little shelf on the wall. It said only five minutes to six. He shut his eyes firmly again. For a little he would luxuriate in his thoughts, undisturbed even by wifely inquiries.

How he had made those dog-faced creatures stir. He felt again the pliancy of the long whippy branch as he had sent the neat leaves at its tip flipping and flapping among the hunched bat bodies. Oh, and then that thin-drawn creak as the branch had finally parted. And hanging there before it had gone with that little notebook skittering down his back.

The notebook. A sudden terrible flush of shame overcame him. All those neatly tabled figures had been something medical. One column had been headed "Pat. No." for "Patient Number" no doubt and there had been a column for temperatures and a column headed "BP" which would be "Blood Pressure." The book was the working notes of some medical research project and he had, through sheer forgetfulness, kept it in the back pocket of those old trousers for nearly seven months.

And the dates. The dates in it had gone back four years. There was four years work there, and he had done nothing about tracing the stiff-looking woman in the dull grey-and-blue sari that it had belonged to.

But things had happened so swiftly just after that incident. Mr. Rao had spoken to him only a few minutes later and next day he had been in the Bats. And since then life had seemed to spiral on and on in a rising tide of work and of ever-thickening suspicions. It had gone on, without a pause it seemed, until he had come to this point, flung off the ever-speeding wheel, his resignation handed in, broken, beaten by black suspicion.

No wonder all thought had vanished of that little leather notebook thrust so hurriedly into the back pocket of those trousers he was not to wear again for so long. But he had thought of it now. He knew now just how important it was.

Was it possible that the woman who had lost it had left traces? There might be a note somewhere of inquiries she had made. A name and address.

He flung himself out of bed and, careless of various jabbing pains, hobbled to the telephone. It was really too early in the day but he could not sit and wait. So he rang every police station where it was likely the notebook's owner would have made inquiries and he shouted at and bullied men on night duty. Soon he was speaking to day-duty desk sergeants and finding them very much put out having to get to work so promptly. But relentlessly he made sure that the appropriate logbooks were looked up, even asking to have all the entries read aloud to him. He shamelessly abused his position to get results, sonorously mouthing again and again the words Black-money and Allied Transactions Squad.

But nowhere did he find any record of anyone having inquired for a lost notebook containing medical research figures.

"Husbandji, what is this you are telephoning?"

Protima had asked the question before. But he had shushed her down. Now there was no reason to do so any more. His last resource had been exhausted. He told her what the matter was.

"But you must find out who that doctor is," she said at the end of his recital, with that fine disregard for impossibilities that was apt to sweep through her when she believed something ought to be done.

The attitude nettled Ghote now.

"It is all very well to say must," he snapped. "But what more can I do?"

"What more? You are asking me? I am not detective. It is you who are that. You should know how to act in a case of this sort."

"I tell you I have done everything that can be done. And now I must get dressed and go to the office."

"Office? You are not going."

"But I must go. I may have resigned, but I have my time to work out."

"If you go, they will find something useless only for you to do. Figures and statistics. But that notebook is important. A child's life may depend on it."

"But— But—"

Ghote thought of trying to explain that the figures in the notebook might not be such that they would save a life at all, let alone that of a child. He thought of pointing out that it was after all possible that all the figures in the book had already been copied out elsewhere, though since the latest dates there had been for only a day or two before he had found it he knew this was perhaps unlikely. He thought of saying that there was nothing in any case he could do to find the notebook's owner even if he did neglect his strict duty and stay away from the office. It was true enough, he conceded, that there was nothing there for him to do now. The Bats had no major operation in hand and, worse, he himself had no least clue towards finding whether one of their number was more likely to have betrayed them than any other.

But he knew that reasoned explanation with qualifications and excuses would be mere waste of breath. No ears were deafer than Protima's when she had made up her mind over something like this.

"But I cannot just not report at office," he said, with a lameness that sounded even to him pathetic.

Protima allowed herself a smile of glinting triumph.

"But you have severely strained ankle," she said. "If you do not telephone that DSP of yours and tell him that, I will."

A vision came into Ghote's mind of Protima telling DSK Naik at length about his ankle, about how he had climbed the neem tree, about how frightened she had been of the bats, about Inspector Radwan and what that fearful Muslim had promised to do. He knew he was beaten.

"Very well, I will ring office myself," he said. "But still I cannot see what more I can do about this notebook."

"You are detective officer," Protima replied. "How many times have I heard you tell that a detective officer does not give up?"

Again he wanted to argue. He wanted to point out in a reasonable manner that he had never actually used such words. But on the other hand it was true that time and again he had acted as if he believed them. So what would be the point of telling her yet once more that everything possible had been done?

So he said nothing and consented to eat the large late breakfast that Protima apparently considered a necessary winding-up process for whatever great leap forward he was going to make. And, a little to his internal chagrin, it was with a stomach comfortably full of crisp puffy puris sent down with well-fried slices of green-fleshed, purple-skinned brinjals that he realised there was at least one more thing he could do to trace the notebook's owner. He could subject the whole little fat volume to a minute page-by-page examination.

He had flicked through it all before to see if anywhere there was a scrawled name. But he had not read every one of those columns and columns of figures to see if anything in them might provide some tiny clue. So now he sat himself down and began to do just that.

This was the sort of work he was thoroughly used to, he reflected with a feeling of comfort, as he progressed. How often on some case or other had he had to plough through a great mass of documents. He had generally known well that, as likely as not, there would be nothing in them that would help. Often he had had no inkling of how anything he might find could help. But nonetheless he had done the hard work because it was there to be done and might reveal in the end the one small fact that would clinch the matter when it came to court. There had been times in plenty when there had been nothing there. There had been times, though, occasionally when there had been something. And there had been enough of the latter for him to have made it a rule with himself never to neglect the search, especially perhaps if it meant hours of dull and laborious effort.

And how different this was, he thought happily, from what had until so lately been the essence of all his waking life: the constant urging on of suspicion. Nothing to suspect here: only these tiny pencilled facts to be examined one after the other for what they were. No asking oneself now "Is the DSP doing this for the very opposite reason that he would appear to be?" No saying "Dear Dayabhai chose to put it that way, did he really mean something quite different?" No poking and prying into every word Radwan uttered to see if one rang false. No weighing Kelkar against Nadkarni, Nadkarni against Kelkar. No, this was the pure art of seeking out only what was there for the alert eye to see.

It was not until the middle of the afternoon that his labours got their reward. Three letters. Three letters and one small word written in the tiniest of scripts towards the end of the book above a group of recordings applying to Patient No 367.

Per F. D'M

But they conveyed a great deal to him. Plainly the woman doctor who had dropped the notebook had had at this point in her research programme some assistance from someone else. She had used that person's figures and had entered them as coming "per" that person. But that was not all. Those initials were significant. That apostrophe between the D and the M meant almost certainly a Goan name, common enough in Bombay. But that particular combination was not so common: more than likely it indicated the name D'Mello.

He ran to the telephone and snatched up the telephone book. Yes, one supposition confirmed. There were no other names in it beginning with D'M than D'Mello. But there was no Dr. F. D'Mello.

Well, researchers worked in hospitals more often than not. He hitched up a chair from its place tucked into the old cane-edged table and began dialling. He took the most obvious places first, Grant Medical College, the JJ Hospital, St. George's, the Gokaldas Tejpal, the KEM, the DM Petit. Then he went on to less obvious places. And at last he found that only one possibility stood between him and the end of what had seemed such a promising trail.

For a few moments he let his hot and sticky hand hover irresolutely above the telephone receiver. But the only thing to do was to ring and find out. He picked up the receiver and dialled those last six figures. For once there were no complications. No wrong numbers. No total silences. No ringing and ringing without any answer. No sudden switching in to someone else's conversation. Just a brisk and lively reply.

"Good morning," he answered. "I wish to speak to Dr. D'Mello, Dr. F. D'Mello."

"Sorry, caller, we have no Dr. D'Mello."

"Wait. Wait. You are sure? No Dr. F. D'Mello?"

"Caller, I have a list in front of me with all the doctors in the hospital. It was brought up to date as of the nineteenth of this month. And that is yesterday."

"Yes," Ghote agreed miserably. "Yesterday."

He put down the receiver.

Well, there was nowhere else for him to go in the hunt now. He had failed. The thought was like gritty ashes under his tongue. Protima had said that he was a detective and would solve this mystery, but he had not succeeded. Was he perhaps truly not a detective after all? Was it really right that he should be resigning?

No, he found himself subduedly trumpeting. No, he was a detective. He was. In his deepest self, despite every failure, despite this setback, despite the enormously greater setback of his failure to find the traitor in the Bats, he was a detective. He was. He was.

And at once his answer came into his head.

He said it aloud.

"All the doctors in the hospital."

That was what that coolly insolent voice had said just now. "In the hospital."

He turned back to the telephone and began going through his list of calls again starting from the end.

"Excuse me, I was putting inquiries earlier about a Dr. D'Mello. Yes, yes. I know. You were most helpful. But there was one thing I forgot to ask. It is this: is your research department considered as separate from the hospital? Do doctors working there come on a different list?"

The fourth call found his man.

Dr. D'Mello did not want to see Ghote. He was busy, a message came back, with an experiment. But when Ghote, after a good deal in insistence, had him sent up a note saying that a set of research figures lost some seven months ago had come into his possession the man himself came running down to where Ghote was waiting. His yellowish Goan features were glowing with excitement. He jerked open the fat little notebook and peered hard at the first page his eyes lit on.

He turned to Ghote.

"Yes, yes. This is Dr. Vijaya Savant's work. My dear fellow, when she thought she would never find these figures again she gave up her research post. She is doing some appalling locum work now. It was nearly the end of her life."

Half an hour later Ghote presented himself at Dr. Savant's modest flat behind the Natraj Hotel in Vir Nariman Road. But it appeared his difficulties were not yet over. Dr. Savant's husband answered the door. Ghote, unthinkingly, first introduced himself with his police rank. And at once Mr. Savant, who, it transpired, ran a business from the flat as an import-export agent for unspecified goods, began to puff out an almost impenetrable wall of evasions and excuses.

He was not sure whether his wife was in. He was not sure where she was. He even began to cast doubts on whether Dr. Savant was his wife at all.

Black money, Ghote thought with mild weariness. No doubt the fellow runs his business largely on black money. Certainly some of the goods he handles will have been smuggled, small quantities of lurex nylon yarn, a few occasional crates of whisky or rum. But a small-time operator if ever there was one.

Relentlessly he stamped on each evasion. Time and again he repeated that he was not at all interested in Mr. Savant's business but only wished to hand back to his wife some property she had lost. And at last he succeeded in driving the fellow up the stairs in front of him.

It was when he looked upwards as they progressed that he knew that his hunt was indeed near its end. The old grey trousers that he saw lumbering up the stone stairs in front of him were the very same elephant-like pair he had seen on Ganpati Day when they had so nearly fallen victim to Moti Chiplunkar's thin skilled fingers. He remembered them with extraordinary vividness. Only this time the wallet jammed in the back pocket was not at all thick.

He smiled to himself. On Ganpati Day he had been looking at, there could hardly be any doubt about it, a wallet crammed with the temporary proceeds of some quick black-money deal. That was what he had saved for the fellow by his grabbing of Moti Chiplunkar. Ah, well.

Then Mr. Savant called out to his wife. And then Ghote held out to her the little, fat, leather-covered notebook. And then there were tears, tears of unrestrained joy.

"I— I never thought I would see it again," the doctor at last managed to say.

"I regret through an oversight—"

But she waved down what Ghote had been going to say.

"How can I thank you?" she babbled. "How can I thank you enough? When I was so careless. So abominably careless on just one day."

She sniffed back a new onset of tears with a noise like water draining away.

"So stupid, so stupid," she went on. "I never put my name in it. But then I never meant to take it out of my working bag. It was only on that Ganpati Day I put it in the basket. But— But— But you must take something to drink. Will you have coffee? Or tea? Shall I make tea?"

"Some coffee would be very pleasant," Ghote said.

Dr. Savant darted into the kitchen of the flat, dabbing at her eyes with the corner of her sari. Her husband, flattened for all his size against a wall, looked at Ghote sullenly and said not a word.

"But how was it you found out it belonged to me?" Dr. Savant called.

Ghote, feeling a little ridiculous under Mr. Savant's mutinous glare, shouted back the answer.

In a little while the doctor came back in, holding a jug down the side of which there was a thick brown trickle of spilt coffee. She was radiant now, her eyes shining with pleasure. When she put the jug down she was unable to stop herself, staid figure though she was, from executing a couple of little dancing steps.

"F. D'M," she said. "That was brilliant, Inspector. A most brilliant piece of work. I only wrote the letters in the book once, when I was ill and Frank volunteered to take some readings for me. Oh, Inspector, do you realise? Do you realise?"

"Well, I am not quite sure . . ."

"Inspector, I shall be able to complete my research project now. I shall be able to give up this wretched locum work and go back to the laboratory. In six months I shall publish. It is wonderful. Wonderful."

"I am delighted to hear," Ghote said.

And he found that indeed he was. He had caught the joy from Dr. Savant, caught a bad case of it. It swept through him now again and again in great irresistible waves. Everything in this world was marvellous. By a miracle the lost figures, all the years of work, had been restored to their proper owner. And soon they would make their impact. Save lives. Defeat misery.

But no, it was not a miracle. By God, it was not a miracle. It was his work. It was his piece of pure detection. That was what had put right the things that had gone so wrong. His detection.

He took the coffee that Dr. Savant was offering him and tried to drink but his hand was trembling so much that he could not. He put the cup down with a clink on the old marble-topped table in the middle of the rather shabby room.

"But sit, sit," Dr. Savant said.

"No," Ghote said suddenly. "No, please forgive me, but I must go now. Thank you for the coffee but I must go at once. I have just realised that I have something most important that I have to say. To my wife. Something very important. A change of plan. A long-term change of plan."

XVII

It had come to Ghote as he had watched the joy-bemused fumblings of Dr. Savant that he could not cease to be the sort of person who sometimes straightened out a kink in the world to such wonderful effect. Whatever happened he could not resign from the police.

And, he thought confusedly as he hurried home to tell Protima, it was not in fact going to be all that difficult to withdraw his resignation. The actual letter had still not been written. He had done no more than say to DSP Naik that he intended to leave the force. He could go to him now, this very afternoon—why not this very afternoon?—and tell him that he had said what he had in a moment of depression.

He could even imply that he had had a quarrel with his wife and that that had been the cause. Detectives, working their long hours, called out often at a moment's notice, missing family weddings, breaking cinema dates, were notorious for having matrimonial difficulties. He could easily let it be understood that all his talk of resignation had been no more than the result of trouble with his wife.

Only he had first to tell his wife.

The thought stopped him dead-still in the middle of busy Vir Nariman Road. He stood jostled this way and that by the scores of passers-by. Fat and jowly businessmen with their black-money flats and their black-money deals banged into him. Exchange touts and the tourists who were their prey pushed by him. The hawkers and the pickpockets steered their way round him. And the dozens and dozens of honest people also swept by, the ones who took no part at all in that great dark world of underground finance. He stood among them all and asked himself if he would really be able to go through with his new resolve.

Because Protima was going to take what he wanted to tell her hard. There could be no doubting that. All that he had just been thinking about the wives of detectives, had she not said it to him more times than he could count? Had she not said to him, often, that he put the police before his own wife and his own child? And was it not true? Much as he loved Protima, much as he loved little Ved, it had always been the job that had come first. It was his life, worked into his veins, and there had been nothing he could do about it.

But he had done something about it in the end. He had told Protima that he was resigning. He had given her at last all that she had asked for. Or rather he had given her what she had never asked for once, and had therefore asked for all the more insistently. How could he go to her now and tell her that he was not going to resign after all?

Yet he was going to do it. He was going back to police work. He was going back to it even despite that fearful burden of suspicion that he would have to heave on to his shoulders once more. He was going to take the risk of seeing life forever through clamped-on yellow spectacles. He knew he could not do otherwise, even if some day in the future it might mean that he would drive his only son away from him in a new outburst of causeless suspicion more deep-going even than that terrible business over the cricket fee.

He would submit to the thrall. And he must tell Protima. At once.

It was a measure of his determination that he hailed a taxi there and then. If he was not going to be out of a job at the end of the month he could afford such occasional luxuries.

But he told the driver to put him down at the end of the road and he walked up towards the house with leaden feet. When he reached the gate he stood with his hand on the bolt that fastened it for as much as a full minute. Then he squared his shoulders and marched in.

He found Protima sitting sewing. A sari was spread in a swirl of soft green and echoing brown all over her lap and she was mending a little tear in its hem.

"Well," she said, "did you get the notebook to whoever it belonged to? Tell me all about it."

Briefly he told her. She looked up at him, limpid-eyed.

"I knew you would do it. I said that you were a real detective."

He stood there, unable to move. No better moment for saying what he had to could have been thrown in his path.

"I— I— I am very thirsty. I must go and get some water to drink."

He headed for the tap in the kitchen. But at the doorway he stopped and turned.

"There is something I must tell."

"Yes? What is it?"

Why had he spoken? Could he not take the words back?

She was looking at him, fondly, trustingly.

He swallowed.

"I do not want to resign."

It was said. Let the heavens fall.

The green and brown sari with the half-mended tear in its hem swirled off her lap and slid in a wide fan on to the floor. The needle with the length of brown cotton in it was let drop. Anywhere. Where it could be trodden by a bare foot, cause trouble, get lost. And Protima, like a dart of fire, had flung herself across the room and had slipped in one lithe movement huggingly close to him.

He was astonished. Speechless.

She looked up at him.

"Oh," she said, "now he is back, truly back."

"Back? Who is back?"

"My husband. The husband I married. Inspector Ghote. My Inspector Ghote is back."

Inspector Ghote—Inspector Ghote now for as long as he still had the strength and ability to go on working—felt as if he had been picked up and transferred bodily to another planet. The world looked different. Everything in it looked different.

They had talked for a little after he had made his reluctant announcement and received Protima's altogether unexpected response. They had talked about anything and everything. The need to get a new fan to replace the old grunting one that would keep jamming and having to be shaken and coaxed into going again. His ankle and the fact that he had hardly noticed it paining him on the way to Dr. Savant's flat and back home again afterwards.

Mr. Savant and his laughably obvious fears over his black-money dealings when there was a police officer unexpectedly on the premises.

Then Protima had suddenly realised that at any moment Ved would be back from school and she had hurried into the kitchen. Soon the house had been full of the tempting smell of something spicy frying.

Ghote sat there sniffing it and letting the thoughts drift through his head like big, castle-piled white clouds. Bit by bit he got round to considering the immediate practical effects of the withdrawal of his resignation.

Did it mean that he would stay with the Bats? If so, he ought to tell Mr. Rao of his decision. No doubt, rather than undergo the complications of infiltrating someone else into the Squad, Mr. Rao would prefer to keep on using him. But did he want to go back to that hated prying into his colleagues' every word and action?

Yes, he did.

It surprised him to find the answer was clear in his mind. But it was there, rock-like. The task was no longer hateful. He wanted to find that traitor in their midst and to do so he was willing to suspect any of them.

But it would not be the same suspicion as before. He could see that now.

Yes, it was what Mr. Rao himself had said to him at Churchgate Station. Those last words he had called out as he had left. Words that had seemed more or less comprehensible at the time, but which only now did he see for what they really were. Remember fire and water, Mr. Rao had said. Neither of those should be let get out of hand. And that was precisely what suspicions had done with him, though not till now had he properly seen it. But he had let them become his master, just as fire and water could be let become bad masters when they ought to be only good servants.

He could see it now. He could see it now that he was in this different world, which, surely, was the world as it had once been. It was the world in which he had had a purpose and that purpose had been backed by the love of a wife and the edifice round him of family life.

The new insight had come step by step. First there had been his climb of the neem tree and its showing him Protima's true feelings. And then, better even than that, there had been this sudden revelation that she not only loved him as a wife but that she wanted him to go on being what he was, a police officer.

In that at last totally clear light he could see.

In that light he wanted now coolly to penetrate the layers of deceit put up by the one of them in the Bats who time and again had warned black-money seths that the net was closing on them. There was one of them benefitting financially to a huge extent from betraying the whole police machine. If there was anything he could do towards exposing that person, whoever it might turn out to be, he was going to do it.

And in the end they would be caught. He had faith that this was so. No one was going to be so clever as to get away with such a betrayal.

Not Inspector Nadkarni, beloved mentor of old, however patient he might be in accumulating a secret source of wealth for his retirement. Not Inspector Kelkar, paragon of the very best in police methods, not however dynamic his methods of cutting through the checks and blocks set up to prevent corruption. Not poor goose-like Dayabhai Patel, sharer of so much learning and humiliation in days gone by, not however tightly gripped he might be by some ruthless and efficient underworld blackmailer. Not Rohit Radwan, for all the contemptuous confidence he might have that there could be no one astute enough to catch him.

And, confronting this picture of the last of his colleagues, a thought came to Ghote, a little nagging reminder of some small piece of unfinished business. He got up and went idly through into the kitchen.

Protima was bent over her stove, transferring with quick deftness two crisp and golden samosas from the ghee-smoking pan to a plate. Ved would come through the garden gate at any moment. Ghote looked at her curved back and elegantly poised head.

"You never cared one button only about Rohit Radwan," he said, in the same bee-meandering tone of their talk earlier.

"Hm?" she answered, busy lifting the second samosa.

"Rohit Radwan," he repeated.

The samosa safely on the plate, Protima straightened up and

turned to him. A look of darting mischief came into her eyes. She gave a little giggle.

"Oh, Husbandji," she said, "you were so easy to tease."

Ghote grinned ruefully.

"You were so far away from me," Protima went on. "With your Bats duty this and your Bats duty that. And those other secret duties that made you always so bad-tempered. I could not help taking advantage of that awful Muslim and his way of thinking that every woman must be in love with him the moment she saw that beard he oils and combs so carefully."

"Yes," Ghote said. "It is a ridiculous beard. Altogether ridiculous."

He stood half watching Protima as she busied herself washing the bowls and spoon she had used for putting together the samosas.

Ved came bursting in and without paying much attention to either of them seized the plate and began eating. Ghote stayed where he was, leaning against the wall of the low-roofed little kitchen. And, piece by piece, he put a picture together in his mind.

"Well," he said at last, suddenly breaking his long silence, "I am sorry to tell I must go out now. It is more of those secret duties."

Protima whirled on him with a look of reproach, though a mild enough one.

He gave her a small smile.

"But," he said, "I am beginning to think that quite soon secret duties will come to an end."

He left her then. But he did not go from the house until he had first quickly consulted a much-folded copy of the Department of Tourism Bombay Guide-Map and had then taken a sheet from the ordinary notepad they kept and had scrawled on it in crude capitals a message.

MR. RAO. POLICE PIG. BEFORE 12 O'CLOCK NOON PIP EMMA TOMORROW I WILL KILL YOU WITH 100 STABS. A FRIEND.

Well before the rendezvous hour of noon next day Ghote entered the Prince of Wales Museum, the huge-domed, many-pinnacled, yellow and grey building that stands in the heart of Bombay surrounded by traffic-mad roads on all sides and protecting from them a wide tree-dotted lawn. It is a landmark, No 100 on the Guide-Map published by the Department of Tourism.

Ghote did not know the interior of the building and he wanted plenty of time to select somewhere well out of range of any solemnly promenading visitors for his conference with Mr. Rao. What he had to say to him must not in the least detail be overheard.

At first he began to doubt whether in choosing the museum for what he hoped would be his last meeting with Mr. Rao had not been unwise. There were many more people about than he had thought, in his own somewhat intimidated attitude to the place, at all likely. Everywhere in the first rooms there were earnest culture-imbibers gazing up at large mournful European paintings or peering with intensity at gay little Rajput and Moghul scenes. He moved on to the huge archaeological rooms. But things were no better there. He stood in the shelter of several of the frequent massive sculptures of many-armed Siva to see whether he remained alone. But each time he did so pairs of European tourists—would that be German they were speaking or French?—came up and almost shoulder to with him pointed out to each other the beauties of the work. In the dark corners where he tried to lurk children, escaped from the vigilance of mother or ayah, would come up and pay more attention to him than to the vast works of art all round.

But at last he found the wing of the great building that was devoted to Natural History, and for some reason there it was almost entirely deserted. Yes, he thought, all I have to do is to stand looking at one of those panoramas behind their big windows and Mr. Rao will sooner or later find me. And then we can start quietly to talk and no one will be near enough to hear a word.

He looked at his watch. It was still only five minutes to twelve.

Standing facing a scene representing Chital deer in a forest clearing, complete behind its plate glass down to the curling dead leaves littering the soft ground, he went over in his mind the argument he would have to present when Mr. Rao appeared. It was important that he should get it all exactly right. He doubted if, in the whole of the rest of his career, he would ever again talk at such length to anyone as mighty as Mr. Rao. The way he said what he would have to might earn him a corner of good opinion right up there at the topmost heights of the service.

He felt a small tension growing inside him. But he was not too much distressed. What he had to say was of so vital an importance that however well or badly he delivered himself it would not greatly matter.

Another look at his watch. Two minutes to twelve. At any moment that quiet authoritative voice might come from behind him as it had done that day, how long ago it seemed now, on the crowded promenade up above Chowpatty Beach.

He stared hard in front of him. The still scene behind the glass was really an extraordinarily clever piece of work. The sunlight and shadow flecking the sides of the deer were really just as they would be in real life. And the stuffed animals themselves might really be alive, poised on tiny hooves, all alertness, all timidity, ready at the least unaccustomed sound to set off at a bounding pace, the embodiment of life-preserving suspicion.

"Ah. Ghote."

He was unable to prevent himself giving a small convulsive start.

"Yes, sir? Yes, Mr. Rao?"

"You have something to tell me? You've abandoned this resignation business?"

"Yes, sir. But I have more to tell than that, sir."

"Indeed? Good man. Well, you've chosen an excellent place for it. We'll just stroll along looking at these panoramas and you talk. I've never seen them before. They're very good. I must bring my grandson."

"Yes, sir."

For a fleeting moment Ghote thought that he too would bring Ved one day to see these forest, jungle and desert scenes from all over India. They were good indeed, painstaking and truthful. Then he began making his prepared statement.

"Sir, you remember that I told you that I thought it must be narrowed down to between Inspector Kelkar, sir, and Inspector Nadkarni?"

"Yes. You told me. And I think your reasoning was excellent."

"Sir, it was not."

"Not?"

Mr. Rao, staring at a twelve-pointed Kashmir Stag (shot, said the notice, by Col RW Burton in the Liddar Valley), looked sharply disconcerted. Ghote hastened to explain. But he was not altogether displeased at seeing that a person as high up as Mr. Rao had accepted the same surface impossibility as he had done himself.

"You remember the circumstances, sir?" he said. "Inspector Nadkarni had kept totally to himself the location of the bungalow out at Juhu where the seth was."

"Yes, yes. He waited until shortly before the raid was made and then informed only those of you actually taking part. I remember."

Ghote silently acknowledged the grasp of distant detail that Mr. Rao had. How important a man of his eminence must have thought that the leak was to have recalled so much.

"Yes, sir," he said. "That was the situation exactly. But do you recall that I mentioned to you also that Sub-Inspector Patel, who was unable to take part in the raid because of stomach trouble, sir, had come into the office also?"

"Yes, I remember. But you told me that he did not appear until after Nadkarni had given the other three of you your briefing."

"Yes, sir. That is so. And I believed for that reason that he could not have known where in Juhu the bungalow was and could not therefore have passed out the information. I could see no reason why any of the three of us who knew should have told him."

"No. There was no reason."

They passed on to look, more or less unseeingly, at a tableau of Black Buck on the Deccan Plateau. Ghote remembered from his police college days at Nasik with Dayabhai Patel seeing animals just like these in the same sort of scenery of dry grass, odd wind-parched trees and cactus plants.

Poor Dayabhai.

"Sir," he said, "although there was no need for either myself or Inspector Kelkar or Inspector Radwan to give Sub-Inspector Patel details of our briefing, one of us did."

"Bad," said Mr. Rao. "Very bad."

He stared with suppressed anger at the still scene on the other side of the big glass pane. One of the bucks was up on its hind legs nibbling at a fruit on a wild-fig tree.

"So it was Patel," he said. "Well, I suppose he was always the most likely. I was never too happy about those stomach indispositions. Altogether too much like a way of creating excuses to get to a telephone."

"Yes, sir, though—"

"Yes, the fundamental trouble with Patel, Ghote, was that he lacked the necessary element of suspiciousness. He was altogether too easy prey for some of the types we have here in Bombay."

"Yes, sir. I am sure that is true, sir. But . . ."

"Yes, man, yes?"

"Sir, it was not Sub-Inspector Patel who betrayed the Bats, sir."

Mr. Rao turned sharply from the Black Buck and looked at Ghote with the beginnings of open anger.

"Sir, Patel was told only so that he could pass on a message, sir. Trustingly, sir."

Ghote swallowed.

"It was like this, sir. And I put a question or two to him this morning that confirmed it. He was asked to pass on a message to a wife. He did it in good faith, sir. But the number he was given to telephone was not that of the wife, sir. It was that of a woman accomplice of some sort."

Damn it, he was spilling it out all the wrong way round. What would Mr. Rao be thinking?

He took a hasty breath.

"Inspector Radwan, sir. It was Inspector Radwan. He asked Daya— He asked Sub-Inspector Patel to pass a message to his wife, telling him she was sick, sir, and was worrying about him. She was sick, sir, it is true. But she was not at home worrying. She had not been at home for many weeks, sir. He had sent her away. To Mahableshwar, sir. Sir, it was only yesterday, when I saw the fellow for the first time in a true light, sir, that I realised the significance of that. An officer on inspector pay could never afford to keep his wife at such a highly respectable hill-station, sir. It is the sort of place you yourself would go to."

"I've been there, Inspector. The golf is excellent. And, of course, I knew that Radwan had sent his wife there. At one time I almost made a move on the strength of it. But then you came along with your ingenious theory narrowing things down to Nadkarni and Kelkar."

"Sir, I am sorry, sir. Sir, it was—"

"That's all right, Ghote. I had the same facts at my disposal as yourself, and I came to just the same conclusion. And I don't think there was anything else against Radwan."

Ghote bit at the inside of his bottom lip.

"Well, yes, sir, there were other things," he said. "But small things only, sir. When I saw the fellow clearly, sir—I had been somewhat prejudiced against him, for domestic reasons, sir—I realised the significance of one or two other small matters, sir. That it was at his recommendation that Sub-Inspector Patel joined the Squad, sir, for instance."

"Yes, you're right. You think he had him in mind for that sort of thing all along?"

"Yes, sir, I think so."

"Yes. Anything else?"

"Well, yes, sir. There was that business at the very start of my tour of duty with the Bats, sir. Radwan tried to mislead me then by giving me a false car number for the gold smugglers' vehicle I was to follow, sir. He also knew the number of the car that I was driving that day, sir, and he must have warned them at the flat in Colaba which we were making for, so that they were enabled to intercept me, sir."

The vision of that "actress" flashed once more into his mind.

"Well, Ghote," Mr. Rao said, "I can see that you have been doing some hard thinking."

"Yes, sir."

"Yes. Thinking hard about every fact you know and testing it till it rings true through and through or shows where it is false. Not easy work, Ghote. But often the only way. Well done."

Ghote felt the two last words booming and reverberating within him as if they were strokes of a great hammer on a heavy bell. Well done. And Mr. Rao had said them. He was rewarded.

"And now, Ghote, I too have an unpleasant duty to perform, over the man, Radwan."

"Yes, sir."

Mr. Rao, tall, lean and grave-faced, turned and walked unhurriedly away out of the dim high room with its rows of brilliantly lit wildlife scenes behind their windows.

For a few unseeing yards Ghote moved on in the direction the two of them had been taking. Then he came to a drifting halt. In front of him, in what for all the world was the jungle round a forest pool in Assam, two tigers were crouched drinking.

But it was not on these powerful and sleek forms that Inspector Ghote's gaze came to rest. It fixed instead on one tiny characteristic detail that the artists had incorporated in their scene. Up in the shadowed branches of one of the trees overhanging the pool there had cunningly been placed the stuffed bodies of a cluster of bats. And they were deep and safely in their noonday sleep.

P